RETURN
TO
HAUNT
THINGS THAT GO BUMP

MELANIE GILBERT

Return to Haunt
Copyright © 2023 by Melanie Gilbert

Scribbling Pen Publishing

Published by Scribbling Pen Publishing
www.scribblingpenpublishing.com

Cover by CReya-tive Book Cover
www.creya-tive.com

Edited by Holmes Editing
www.holmesedits.com

To Heather, for being the best partner-in-crime and business partner. This wouldn't be as fun without you.

CHAPTER 1

Falcon - At the height of Chaos' reign.

C ould Arlo have chosen a more remote place to meet? The Charmer had called this little gathering of the First Four. I could only imagine the topic of discussion would be the calamity raging in the world. Chaos, the last Darken leader, had been aptly named for the discord he created after his birth on this planet. The results of that discord fed my people, Shadows, but Arlo's Charmers wouldn't receive strength from Chaos' dysfunction like I did. As the weakest among us, Arlo likely wanted an accord of some kind.

I slid into a dark recess of the cavern where the other three First Four of the Darken awaited my arrival. Arlo was joined by Elias—the Howler First Four, a hairy man who could change into a human-beast creature—and Oswald—the First Four of the Conjurers, a man who could use magic and had a spell for almost everything. Together, we were called the First Four, the first of our kinds. I was the first of us all.

Chaos had come last. He'd been birthed by darkness not long after Arlo had been created by the lust in the world. Chaos wanted all the power. Not unlike the rest of us. And no different than us, Chaos had no interest in sharing his power. However, unlike the rest of us, Chaos did have the strength to destroy all the Darken.

"Finally you show up." Oswald, a red-haired ugly man, scowled at me. The magic wielder had been our greatest concern before Chaos' creation because of his greed and need for supremacy. I'd been created by the first drop of blood which had been shed on this planet. It must have been some huge act of human darkness which had created Chaos. I'd been too trapped in my own lusts to notice his arrival before it was too late. I'd learned my lesson.

"Enough, Oswald." Arlo swayed beside the Conjurer as a whiff of blood reached my senses. My eyes darted down to Arlo's middle where he held a wad of rags over a profusely bleeding wound. The Charmer shrugged. "Death took a swing at me, but I'm still standing."

"Not for long with that wound the way it is." I glared at Oswald. "You could help him with that, you know."

"And why should I?" Oswald's crooked, nasty teeth almost made me shiver in disgust. How had this man sired children? How desperate did a woman have to be to allow him to impregnate her? I nearly shivered at the thought. At least Arlo was a handsome man, a trait his children had gained from him.

"With Arlo's death," Elias, the Howler, answered, "Chaos will grow stronger. He'll come after the rest of us soon enough afterward. Arlo is weak. Everyone knows this. His people thrive on the effects of sex. During this time of, well, chaos, the Charmers are weakening. They don't fight. Their powers are useless against Chaos' minions."

"Thanks for laying it all out there." Arlo glowered at the hairy man beside him. Elias wasn't much more handsome than Oswald, but Howlers preferred to reproduce within their own people. That was a trait which would lead to their demise as more Howlers were killed at Chaos' children's hands.

"It's the truth, and you know it, Charmer." Elias waited for Arlo to nod before forging on. "Next, Chaos will go after either Oswald or myself. He'll save Falcon for last. Chaos fears the Shadows more than the rest of us, because his discord serves them as much as it does himself."

Oswald's eyes narrowed further. He hated me the most for the same reason as Chaos: as the oldest, I was the most powerful of the four of us in the cavern. Oswald wanted that power, and he loathed Chaos' arrival into this world more than the rest of us because Chaos held the power Oswald wanted over Elias, Arlo, and me. Without Chaos, Oswald believed he had a chance to overthrow me, murder me, and send me to whatever hell awaited my kind. Considering I'd been born from darkness, I didn't expect to go anywhere else. If I even had a soul.

"If we don't do something," Arlo gasped out, "we're all doomed. We've fought each other since our creations. For once, we need to work together, or Chaos wins." His face tightened in a cringe filled with pain.

Arlo had ordered his people to kill me countless times— never coming after me himself—but I'd never responded to those attempts. The man was the weakest of us all, and he knew it. He lived by the motto that if he killed me first, I couldn't kill him. I had no interest in killing Arlo, though. Charmers, because of their promiscuity, outnumbered the rest of us. In a battle, Arlo's numbers would come in handy, whether that battle was against Chaos or Oswald. Though, only if Arlo allied to my side of the war.

From what had been said, it seemed as if Arlo and Elias didn't know about the information the Conjurer had. I did. Rather, the two hadn't called him out on his knowledge like I planned to. I smirked. "Oswald, I know you've been working on a spell to entrap Chaos, but it's not powerful enough yet."

"You spied on me—"

"Shut up. I know for a fact you've been spying on me since you were created. I've allowed you to see what I wanted." Oswald's face turned as red as his hair. His anger humored me. However, I didn't goad Oswald further. As much as I hated to admit it, we needed the Conjurer's magic. "Arlo is right. If we all wish to survive this, and I know we all have our self-preservation at heart, then we need to work together. Alone, we're not strong enough to face Chaos and win. Even if we used all of our people. A fight with him would prove to be a bloodbath."

"Something you wouldn't mind, Falcon." Oswald grinned at me. "Blood strengthens you, does it not?"

A sneer curled my lips. "Along with fear, or did you forget that, Conjurer? You reek of terror, so don't pretend Chaos doesn't frighten you. At least Arlo isn't trying to hide his emotions behind a fake facade." I turned to Elias. "You, however, are entirely too calm."

"I've been presented with a deal." Elias' admission took even me by surprise. The spies I had monitoring Elias hadn't told me this.

"What kind of deal?" Arlo stumbled back and fell on his butt. We needed to hurry this along, or we'd lose the man.

"My people aren't as affected by this in a negative way," Elias admitted. "Chaos has given us an abundance of flesh to eat, and he isn't threatened by my kind. We prefer to roam like animals. If I deliver the three of you to him, he'll allow my people to live as beasts."

"It's a lie." Arlo, pale as a cloud on a sunny day, closed his eyes.

"I know that," Elias growled and nodded toward Arlo. "Oswald, save the man, or risk Falcon and me tearing you apart. This is ridiculous."

Oswald rolled his eyes and crouched beside Arlo. The Charmer, with his brown curly hair, barely breathed. Oswald's spell was whispered, like he feared Elias and I would copy his words even though we didn't have magic or access to his Conjurers for them to replicate the spell—an insightful idea I would dwell on at a later date.

With the spell cast, Arlo's breathing evened out. Oswald stood once more. "He'll regain consciousness in time. For now, let's talk about how to use our combined powers to imprison Chaos. I highly doubt we can kill him."

"It's unlikely," Elias agreed. "He's too strong, and his powers are too unpredictable."

"One thing also remains to be considered," I added. "If it

takes all of us to imprison him, our powers will act as his prison, if I understand magic at all. Am I correct?" I mainly looked to Oswald who knew the magic we'd need to use. He nodded, a sour expression marring his already ugly face. "Then, should one of us die at a later date…"

Oswald groaned, hating to admit this truth. "The spell will falter and free Chaos."

"So, we need to make sure we don't die." Elias spoke the words as if staying alive would be easy. Assassination attempts from the other First Four weren't the only threats to our lives. Our people were eager to destroy us. It seemed all Darken were in love with power.

"Our people, especially mine and Falcon's, grow too strong." Oswald's thoughts seemed to be along the same path as my own. "To keep them from overpowering us, we'll need to implement a condition."

"They have to die." Arlo stood with a moan. Color had begun to return to his face. If this was all true, the Charmer needed someone at his back, protecting him. With reluctance, I admitted that the best person at his back was me.

Arlo continued as I wove my thoughts into a plan. "If our people grow too powerful, powerful enough to overthrow the four of us, the world will burn, taking the rest of us out. To preserve each of our fates, when our people grow too old, we put them to death. And, we have to keep each other in check. We do not trust each other, a fact we've never hidden, so we'll meet twice a year to check in. We need balance. This is the best way. The only way, really."

We all looked at each other. No one objected. Oswald appeared to have swallowed a burr, but even he didn't oppose the plan. With all the hair covering his face, it was hard to read Elias' expression. Arlo still appeared close to death.

Oswald clapped his hands together. "Well, let's get started, shall we?"

CHAPTER 2

Brina - Present Day

I held my breath. Falcon's declaration about all of us dying punched me in the gut, making it hard to breathe. He really had no hope for us?

"Chaos can't die?" My eyes bounced back and forth between the First Four—Elias, the Howler; Arlo, the Charmer; and Falcon, my mate and Shadow. Err, First Three? Oswald the Conjurer was dead. Which knowledge led me to ask, "How can a Darken not die?"

Arlo glowered at me. "Dear Brina, as long as you have been alive, there has been chaos. Can you picture a world without it?"

I cringed. "Not really."

Falcon took my hand and squeezed it. "Chaos is so powerful, so ingrained into this world, he even has constant influence over Phoenixes. And his influence is growing. The humans are the most swayed by him, and it shows." He sighed. "The Darken and Phoenixes are nearly as bad. There's such a constant influx of discord in the world, the result of which is Chaos' immortality."

"What do we do?" My father Keeve stepped up beside me to join the huddle of Darken. "You all seem to believe there's no hope."

"There is no hope." Arlo flicked a small stone off the top of the walkway. He watched it fly into the night until the darkness hid the stone from his nearly human eyesight. "Phoenixes can't purge Chaos' influence from their lives, as much as I'm sure you would all love to try. It's impossible. Not even goody-goody Brina can do it. Especially since chaos has ruled her life since the time she met Falcon. Of no choice of her own, of course." Arlo smirked and added the last part when I narrowed my eyes at him. His lips fell quickly. "But the truth remains the same: Chaos touches everything. He is so ingrained into this world—making him thousands of times more powerful than he was when he walked the earth—I'm not sure if he could even be imprisoned again. Even if we could manage such a spell."

"So you're giving up? Already? Without a fight?" Righteous indignation burned inside me. My skin began to glow until Falcon wrapped his arm around my waist, his hand resting on my hip.

"Arlo isn't giving up, darling." Arlo rolled his eyes in contradiction to my mate's statement. "The Charmers don't have much hope. They are afraid. Rather, Arlo is afraid for them. His people don't know how much they should fear. Hell's fury, they have much to be afraid of. Chaos will wipe them out in a second."

"Thanks for the reminder," Arlo grumbled beneath his breath as Elias scoffed.

The Howler tried to run his fingers through his hair, but the strands were so matted from years of neglect, his fingers became stuck. He swore and crossed his arms over his massive chest. "I should've taken the deal that monster offered long ago. Would've saved me decades, or even centuries, of misery under Oswald's control."

"You'd be dead if you worked with Chaos before. And I'm sorry," Falcon apologized with a sincerity that twisted my heartstrings. "Had we known Oswald's power had grown so much, Arlo and I would have stopped him. Your past decisions to work with the side more likely to win did not work in your favor."

"No, they did not." Elias leaned against the wall of the walkway. "Though the one time I chose the party with lesser power has come back to bite me." He gnashed his teeth. They were yellow, sharp, and made my skin crawl. Worse, memories of recent deaths began to replay in my mind.

Sensing my fear, Falcon pulled me closer to him. My fear strengthened him, but also every Shadow around would know how afraid I was. They no longer needed to feed on my fear to become strong. Falcon provided them with their energy to survive. I needed to stomp the fear down and be brave. My mate would protect me, and in this life, I could now protect myself. There was no reason to fear Howlers anymore.

"We should regroup in an hour's time," Falcon declared. "Arlo and Elias need to reprimand their people while Felicia needs to announce her new role as First Four to the Conjurers. For simplicity's sake, Felicia will be the Conjurer First Four, the first leader among her people. The title has been around since nearly this world's beginning. Let's not change it now. Keeve, my people will aid yours in rebuilding your compound until the sun grows close to rising. Then my Shadows will return to their home."

Dad turned to face the inner courtyard of the compound. A wall the Conjurers had blown up still crumbled while Phoenixes rushed to brace it. Shadows helped them, giving them enough numbers to succeed. Others helped the injured to their feet or carried them inside for medical care.

My father turned back to Falcon. "I appreciate the assistance. We could use it."

Falcon nodded. "You are family. I will do what I can to help in any way possible."

"Thank you. We can meet in my conference room in an hour. Slide to my office, and I'll direct you to the place."

"Understood."

Arlo disappeared. My improved eyesight allowed me to see him reappear near the line where his Charmers circled the Phoenix compound. As one, the Charmers fell to their knees. For a moment, it appeared as if the quakes announcing Chaos' release had begun again, but my own feet didn't shake. The Charmers huddled together, quivering before their leader.

"He won't hurt them, will he?" I didn't bother whispering to Falcon. Everyone around me had excellent hearing.

"No. During the time of Chaos' turmoil, he probably would have. Not now. You've helped change him for the better nearly as much as you changed me, my darling." Falcon leaned over and placed a kiss to my forehead. "He's far from perfect, but he's improving."

"Good. Adler deserves that."

My son, Quest, groaned. While he was half Phoenix, Quest favored his father's genes and had been raised by an adopted Shadow mother. "I can't believe my sister allowed herself to be courted by a First Four."

Astrid, Quest's long-time love, patted his shoulder, her long gray hair blowing in the breeze. "Don't worry. Arlo knows what will happen to him if Adler so much as gets a papercut in his presence."

"This has been fun." Elias stood and stretched. "Not really, but it's nice to have my mind back. I'll have Arlo return me here as soon as I've taken care of a few things and he's dealt with his people. Good luck to you, Felicia. It was nice to meet you. I hope to see you in an hour."

I blinked rapidly as Elias threw himself over the edge of the wall. Not so much because he'd jumped from a good height—his body could handle the impact—but because of his underlying threat to my Conjurer friend. Now that I had a good look at her, Felicia did appear pale.

"Take Cash with you, Felicia," Falcon ordered. "Keep him as long as you need."

"Thank you, Falcon." Felicia smoothed her shirt out and gave him a strained smile. "All will be well. Cash will return me here in an hour. Brina," she smiled at me, "thank you for saving us."

"It wasn't just me."

"No, but no one else could have commanded a mixed army of Phoenix and Darken. Even Arlo obeyed you. Thank you."

Felicia didn't startle when her Shadow guard Cash appeared at her side. The two took hands and disappeared as Arlo had, sliding from shadow to shadow in the darkness.

"Will Felicia be okay?" Turning, I watched the field for her and Cash. They appeared amongst the Conjurers, near the place where Oswald's body had burned. Falcon and I had changed into fiery birds, had soared together across the sky, and as one, had flown through Oswald, igniting him.

Falcon let out a heavy sigh as he, too, watched the field. "The Conjurers taste freedom for the first time in…ever. They've lived in terror for generations. They don't wish to be governed. Not by someone who fled and came to me for protection. As much as I couldn't put Circe in charge of them because she's too close to me, Felicia will have the same problem with the Conjurer's perceptions. They'll think I'm ruling them."

"But is there a better choice?"

"None that I know of. Oswald kept his people separated from the rest of us as much as possible. I have no doubt he killed his people much younger than Arlo, Elias, and I did to keep them from overthrowing him. Hopefully the Conjurers will give Felicia a chance and discover they don't have to spend the rest of their lives living in fear of their leader. They only need to fear Chaos." Falcon shrugged. "In which case, their fear will be short-lived."

I straightened my back as a humming filled the air. The sound came from Arlo. In fact, he wasn't humming. He was singing, but from this distance, I couldn't make out the words. He had a beautiful voice, though. The tune was hypnotic. It silenced a moment later when all the Charmers slid from the field.

"His voice was their command to obey him," Falcon explained for me and those around us. "No matter where they are, his Charmers will hear him and obey."

"Why didn't that work before? Just the fear of Oswald?"

Falcon shook his head. "They should have obeyed. Oswald must have hampered Arlo's magic as he did our ability to slide. Curses be, he's destroyed us right beneath our noses."

Squeezing Falcon's hand, I tried to give him a hopeful smile. "At least I have my memories back." My brows furrowed. "Well, most of them. There are gaps where I recall nothing."

Dad nodded. "You were reborn too often without maturing for the memories to not be damaged. Even so, some Phoenixes are reborn with missing memories. Not often, but instances have occurred."

"At least in this, I'm not completely weird."

Falcon squeezed my hand and excused himself to give orders to Hawke and his people. Dad followed suit, along with his second-in-command Noa. The rest of us dispersed as well to aid the Phoenix compound with the aftermath of Oswald's attack, or to clean up for our meeting. Somewhere, Phoenixes had found brooms to sweep up the smaller debris from the wall. How they planned to remove large chunks of the wall, I had no idea and would consider a way to help them. I didn't rule a race of Darken or the Phoenixes. Still, I needed a moment to myself before joining in the cleanup efforts.

Falcon met me by the front door of the compound. Our sons, Astrid, and the rest of my family and friends worked to clear the rubble so the rebuilding could start.

"Rebuilding a wall won't be enough," Falcon mumbled, watching everyone work. "Not in the end."

"I won't give up, Falcon." My eyes burned with anger as I watched Quest and Orion pick up a large rock from the wall, each straining under its weight. They should have been raised together. "I just got my family back. I won't let them go, let you go, without a fight."

My mate lifted my chin with his fingers. Our eyes locked, the stripes around his eyes looking even more ferocious in the night. "I know, Brina. And I will protect my family until the end. But in the meantime, I've begun to realize the error of my ways."

My brows drew down. "Which is?"

"I have relied too much on your memories returning. I've done little to court you in this life."

"Well, you were trying to scare me to death for a while. Then you were attempting to keep me alive. On top of that, we were separated before my memories could kill me. It's been quite a wild ride for us."

Falcon gave a small smile. "It has, but that does not excuse me for assuming your memories would return and everything would be as it once was centuries ago. You are different, Brina. There is still a fierce, unyielding fire within you. That has not changed. But your human life has given you a perspective you did not have before. Before us, you were invincible. Like you said, everyone you knew would be reborn when they were killed. Because of your situation, you value life more than you previously did.

"I've lived forever. Time can dull the senses. You've made me realize I have not taken advantage of the time I've had. So, without assuming that this new you will love me as much as the old you, I will ask if I might have permission to court you?"

I gave a soft laugh. "Falcon, you're my mate. I think the time for courting has passed."

"You are a Phoenix, which you know because that has caused us many a problem since we met, Heaven knows. You're still thinking like a human, but you are not one. Your Phoenix side needs to love me for more than our memories together. You need the assurance that I still care, that I still love you." My smile fell at his reminder.

Yes, I no longer felt like a human, and I had memories from previous lives, but they all seemed so surreal, so...outlandish. The memories played like a movie in my head, like cinematic entertainment. I'd led armies of Phoenixes. Me. The girl who couldn't figure out what to do with the rest of her life. The girl who couldn't hack college. Falcon hit the nail on the head. Balancing my Phoenix life with my most recent human life would take some time.

"You're right. I feel like two distinct people, and yet, I still feel like me." Trying to reconcile everything in my head would give me a headache, so I changed the subject. "I guess I should help out here. I just needed a moment to breathe."

"Why?"

"Uh, because we could have almost died."

"No, Brina, why should you go help in the cleanup efforts?"

"Um, because it's the right thing to do. Plus, you have a very important meeting to go to, and everyone out here could use all the help they can get."

He turned me around by the shoulders and pushed me through the open doorway. "And you think you're not invited to this very important meeting?"

"I'm not a First Four, and I don't lead the Phoenixes."

"You are my mate, my partner in leading the Shadows. If I fall, they will follow you. Now, lead me to your room so we can clean up."

I tugged Falcon to a stop. The light in the hallway didn't harm him as he turned his attention back on me. He was powerful. Stupidly powerful. The rays of the sun would still kill him, but Falcon could withstand all other lights. His Shadows still shrunk away from light and were weakened by it.

His face darkened. "Brina, I do not have a secret plan to woo you. That would take too long, because the next time you're in my bed, I plan to take things nice and slow, reminding you of how perfect we are together." His husky voice had my knees weakening and heart beating wildly.

I cleared my throat so Falcon wouldn't hear the effect he had on me while I spoke. "While I'd love nothing more than for you to try seducing me, we're going the wrong way."

Falcon peered over his shoulder. "We're in the entry. How can we be going the wrong way?"

13

"Because my room isn't here. It's at home."

Falcon's lips were on mine in a blink. Fire burned through me from my head to my toes as I responded to the passion coming from him. If I opened my eyes, I wouldn't be surprised to see the entire compound burning down. His touch was electric, and his taste was perfectly Falcon.

With difficulty, I pulled back from my mate. His black eyes had a tint of red in them, which happened when his emotions were high.

"Conjurers curse it all. Come on," he growled and tugged me farther into the building. "If I take you home now, we'll miss that blasted meeting."

Instead of allowing me to lead the way to my room, Falcon guided me up the stairs to Dad's office. He opened the door without knocking and entered first. When he was sure no danger waited for us, he allowed me inside.

"I thought you wanted me to take you to my room so we could clean up." It didn't miss my attention that he walked across the room to look out the window, and stayed there when he turned around. "Problem?"

Falcon smirked. "Oh, darling, there would have been a problem if I'd taken you anywhere near a bed."

His dark eyes brought heat to my stomach, and I nearly melted on the spot. Thankfully Dad's door opened. Dad entered the room with Noa behind him. Hopefully they couldn't read the situation we were in. That would be so awkward, thinking of my mate in such a way in my dad's office.

"I figured you two would be the last people to arrive. In fact, I had doubts you would even be on time." Dad reached up to unscrew a lightbulb. Noa did likewise. Half the room already had missing bulbs. Apparently, they wanted our Darken allies to feel more comfortable.

Falcon leaned back against the wall behind Dad's desk, crossing his arms over his broad chest. "If we'd left, we would have missed the entire meeting."

My cheeks burned. Did he have no shame? This was my father!

Dad chuckled. "If Sybil and I had been separated as long as the two of you have been, we wouldn't see the light of day for days."

"Dad!" I covered my face. Seriously? Of course, the thoughts Falcon put in my mind started rolling old memories. Thankfully I was saved by Felicia and Cash sliding into the room.

"How accepting are your people?" Falcon jumped straight into business like he and Dad hadn't been sharing laughs seconds ago.

Felicia shook her head. "I'm not strong enough, Falcon. Circe would have been a better choice."

"Do what you can. No one else is as powerful as you."

"Power doesn't matter when so many people want you dead."

Falcon remained grim. "Cash will protect you."

Felicia nodded. "I know he'll do his best, but Shadows are not immune to Conjurer magic, as we've seen, and light is a weakness."

Cash cleared his throat. The young Shadow placed his hand on the small of Felicia's back, giving her comfort. "Falcon, as much as I am honored to protect the First Four of the Conjurers, wouldn't she be better off with an older Shadow? Someone like Hawke would be better than me. Light weakens me more."

"I wish I could," Falcon answered. "I'd order a legion of Shadows to guard her, but I can't. They will never learn to trust Felicia, and they will grow to hate her for subjecting them to Shadows in their lives, like Shadows are the rulers of all the Darken. They will fight her harder if they feel trapped. The Conjurers won't fear a young Shadow as they will an old one. As you said, you weaken easier than someone like Hawke would. However, the same is true for all young Shadows. I can find a replacement—"

"No," Cash cut Falcon off. He stepped slightly closer to Felicia. He didn't seem aware he'd done it. "I will protect Felicia. My concern was only for her safety, not a request to be removed as her guard."

"Understood."

"Brina, why don't you take those who are early for our meeting to the conference room. I've already taken some light-bulbs out. Cash, will walking there hurt you?" Dad's concern for his enemy's comfort was commendable. Not many Phoenixes would care if a Shadow hurt or not.

Cash shook his head. "If it's not far, I'll be fine."

"It's two doors down."

"Then I'll be well. Thank you."

Dad indicated the door. I led Falcon, Felicia, and Cash from the room. Cash's eyes watered, and he ducked his head from the overhead lights. We kept a brisk pace to keep Cash from suffering longer than needed, and I opened the door to a confer-ence room I knew well. This was the room I'd met with the Commanders in. The Commanders remained outside, leading the cleanup efforts.

Cash heaved a sigh as we entered the room. Dad had removed most of the lightbulbs from the ceiling, giving the Shadows plenty of space to be comfortable. If other Phoenixes entered the room, they'd have a mild freakout. Phoenixes grew uneasy with darkness. Their enemies could slide into their compound if any shadows created were big enough. Dad shooting the lights outside nearly gave some heart attacks. I was sure of it.

The room seemed sufficiently dark for the Shadows. While they preferred complete darkness, this wouldn't harm them. If needed, Arlo and any other Charmer could slide in or out of the room.

"Take a seat anywhere. At this table, no one is above another, so your seat's location doesn't matter." I indicated the round table in the center of the room. White boards hung on three walls in the room, while the other wall had a large window which overlooked the damaged courtyard.

"Where does your father usually sit?" Felicia eyed the table, not wanting to break some unspoken rule or a known rule she didn't know about.

"He sits anywhere. Like I said, no one is above another, and there are no assigned seats. Please, sit." To break the ice, I pulled a chair out to sit in. Falcon didn't seem to approve of my choice in seating because he took my arm and led me to the other side of the table.

"Never put your back to the door," he advised. "Leave that place for your enemies."

"You think this meeting will be uncivil?" Concern twisted my stomach. "Arlo wouldn't do anything. Elias—"

"Will also be decent," Falcon finished. "However, people are scared and stressed. Fear makes people do things they otherwise wouldn't."

He knew that firsthand. He'd pretended to be a monster because my fear made him so much stronger than others', and he needed that strength for his people. Falcon had regrets, but now I understood why he'd done what he had. I couldn't say whether or not I approved of his methods, but I understood why he'd made the choices he had.

Felicia pulled a chair out two spots over from Falcon and nearly collapsed into the seat. The strain of leading already showed with deepening stress lines on her face. Cash took the seat between her and Falcon. While Cash appeared calm, Falcon sucked in a deep breath, scenting Cash's fear. Or was it my fear which strengthened him?

Silence surrounded us as we waited for Dad, Noa, Arlo, and Elias to join us. We'd been early, but as the clock on the wall ticked, everyone began to grow antsy. Felicia tried not to fidget. Cash kept glancing at the clock. Even Falcon had taken my hand and rubbed circles into my palm using his thumb.

"What if they're not coming?" I asked when the clock indicated we'd been sitting for a half hour past when we were supposed to meet.

"Arlo will come." Falcon's voice held no doubt, and I trusted his judgment. He knew Arlo best. "The Charmers are sitting ducks without the rest of us. Arlo needs our protection and support, though he'll be in for a rude awakening when I force his people to learn to fight. If anything, they can be collateral damage."

"Falcon!"

"It's war, Brina. The battle with Oswald was ugly, but this… this will be beyond anything you can imagine. People will die. People we know and love will die. Most won't be reborn. We might as well die strategically."

"Well, that's one way of looking at it," Felicia grumbled.

The door opened while my mind still fought to comprehend Falcon's words. Arlo entered first, a grim expression on his otherwise handsome face. I froze as a half dozen Howlers entered the room behind him. Dad and Noa entered last. Noa closed the door.

The Howlers appeared to have been in a fight, probably the battle earlier. They stood beside a wall near the door. Cuts and bruises covered whatever skin we could see. Sections of hair had been torn out. Even the females were pretty hairy.

"Where's Elias?" Felicia asked, slowly rising to her feet.

Falcon growled deep in his chest. The tiny hairs on the back of my neck stood up at the sound. "He isn't coming. Elias is siding with Chaos. Shadows scare him to death. That idiot hasn't changed a bit."

The largest Howler male shook his head. "It's worse than that. I'm not sure about Elias or what he's doing, but we were attacked."

"I can see that."

"No, Falc." Arlo ran shaking hands through his curly hair. "It was Chaos. When I slid to the place where Elias and I were to meet, I was met by death and these six. They could very well be the last Howlers on the planet. Before, none of us would've cared too much—except to keep the balance—but now we're at even more of a disadvantage."

Howlers terrified me. Those six could tear me apart with ease. I had many memories to prove it. However, these Howlers seemed more afraid of us than we should be of them. Two female Howlers huddled close together. Like the men, their clothes were torn and dirty. Their blood covered rips in the cloth.

The largest who seemed to lead the group spoke up again. "Yes, Elias mentioned working with Chaos before the attack. I'm not sure what he meant."

"What's your name?" Falcon asked the Howler.

"Garrett, sir." Garrett bowed his head slightly to the First of the Darken. While I'd grown comfortable and relaxed around Falcon, others still feared him. These Howlers were no different.

"Keeve, do you have a place for these young Howlers to clean up?" Falcon indicated the group.

Dad slapped Noa on the back of the shoulder. "Noa will take you to the infirmary where your wounds can be looked at and new clothes given to you." The Howlers huddled closer together. Dad gave them a soft smile. "You are safe here. No one will harm you. Especially with Noa watching over you. I know that doesn't seem likely, but I keep my word."

"Thank you, sir." Garrett gave Dad a head bow as he had Falcon. "We are grateful for your kindness in our hour of need. Especially after what happened tonight. We are enemies and have killed many of your people."

"Oswald is dead. Those forced to follow his orders should not be punished for the Conjurer's sins. My Phoenixes have killed many of your Howlers as well. Darkness never breeds light. Maybe it's time for us to take a look at our ways as well." Dad opened the door and ushered the group out. The females wouldn't look at anyone as they left.

"Do you think they're telling the truth?" Felicia asked, sliding back into her seat. "Not about the attack, but wanting help from us? Or could they be here to trick us somehow?"

Arlo shook his head and sat beside me. Dad sat beside Felicia, leaving half the seats on the other side of the circular table empty.

Arlo remained grim as he answered Felicia. "They are genuinely terrified. Whatever happened, it scared them enough to beg me, their enemy, for help and safety. The attack killed hundreds, if not thousands, of Howlers. Their dead bodies are scattered all over the ground where I was to meet Elias."

"Was Elias' body there?" Falcon asked.

"No. I searched for him. He was nowhere in sight. Whatever happened, his people paid a high price for his stupidity."

A deeper darkness seemed to settle over the room. Falcon and Arlo swore. Goosebumps pricked my skin as a feeling of dread filled my stomach. Could Chaos really destroy an entire race of Darken in such a short amount of time? If so, Falcon and Arlo were right to predict our doom. We would all be dead soon.

A man with white hair and pale skin appeared on the empty side of the table.

"Hello, brothers," Chaos crooned.

CHAPTER 3

Brina

"I t's so good to see you both." Chaos gave a bright smile to Falcon and Arlo who'd both stiffened on either side of me. Chaos' smile wasn't exactly filled with amusement. It had some sort of crazy mixed in. Maybe it was the way his eyes kept changing colors, or the feeling Chaos emitted. He seemed to be off kilter. Well, he certainly wasn't sane.

"I'm afraid Elias won't be joining us for this little homecoming celebration." Chaos tossed Elias' still-bleeding head onto the table and sat down. "Such a pity. Two brothers gone in only a few hours." He smiled wider at the other two Darken. "But I'm so glad the two of you are here. You were always my favorites. Oswald always thought he was better than me. You probably know the feeling, Falcon. And Elias, he was predictable. I mean, Arlo's a bit predictable—he runs at the first sign of danger—but he at least makes his predictability entertaining. Elias broke a promise to me. How very rude."

Chaos sat back, relaxed as if we really were all friends. "Honestly, it is good to see you, brothers. And Falcon, I see you've been lucky while I've been away." Chaos waggled his eyebrows at me. "She looks good with your mark on her. Brina, is it?" He turned to Felicia and Dad. Felicia had paled as if she might throw up. "And you're Felicia and Keeve. It is so good to meet you as well!"

"We're not brothers, Chaos," Falcon interrupted. I kicked him. He needed to play nice with the crazy guy in the room.

Chaos rolled his eyes. "You sound like Oswald, Falcon. Don't tell me he rubbed off on you while I was gone."

By "gone," I could only assume Chaos meant his imprisonment. I wasn't sure which should freak me out more: Elias' head on the table or Chaos' nonchalance about his captivity. I'd expected a roaring monster to show up. Especially after the massacre of the Howlers. I had not expected a man who pretended he'd stepped out for a lengthy vacation and had just returned.

"Now, I realize we didn't quite see eye to eye the last time we were together. So to rectify that, I'm here to offer all of you the same deal I offered Elias long ago. He went back on that deal, and that upset me." If upsetting Chaos ended with Elias' head being cut off, I didn't want to see what more than "upset" meant to the crazy man.

"You want us to join you," Arlo predicted.

"Yes!" Chaos squealed, clapping his hands like a child. The man was nearly jumping in his seat with excitement. Chaos was definitely unhinged. "Can you picture it?" Chaos waved his hand in the air as if he read a banner. "Darken brothers team up with young Conjurer and Phoenix."

Chaos shrugged and leaned back in his chair, his sudden mood change to somber giving me whiplash. "If you don't, I can't guarantee how my children will react to you. The Howlers learned the hard way."

Felicia and I jumped when Chaos slapped the table and jumped to his feet with a large smile. "Well, I best be off. Lots of the world to see now that I've returned. The humans really are delightful, are they not? I best go make some friends. I'll check back in with you later after you've had time to discuss my offer. Though, it's not much of a choice, but etiquette says I should at least let you deliberate over the choices. Toodles!"

Chaos disappeared as quickly as he'd joined us. The tension didn't seep from the room with his absence. In fact, Arlo seemed to grow more and more anxious as time passed. His head kept whipping around as if Chaos would re-emerge out of thin air and take Arlo's head off this time.

Felicia cleared her throat, breaking the overbearing silence. "So, now what?"

"He slides like us?" Cash's eyes didn't stray from the chair Chaos had sat in.

"No," Falcon answered. Arlo seemed to struggle to find his voice, or even stop looking around. "Chaos is unpredictable. He travels how he wants. He appears where he wants. Darkness or light, it doesn't matter."

"How do we beat an enemy who could drop into the middle of our army and destroy us from within?" Cash's question was the one I'd begun to ask myself. "I see why you've predicted our demise so fervently. He's crazy. Crazy and powerful."

"Arlo," Falcon called, gaining the Charmer's attention. "He's not coming back. Not yet."

Arlo stood so fast his chair tipped backwards. "If you'll excuse me, there's something I need to take care of. I'll return momentarily." He disappeared before anyone could comment on his declaration.

"He's coming back, right?" I turned to Falcon who nodded.

"I'm not sure what he's doing, but I have an idea. Arlo has every right to be afraid. When we first trapped Chaos, Arlo and I were enemies just like the others. He showed up to our meeting, the one where we discussed how to stop Chaos, with blood pouring from his gut. If we hadn't needed Arlo, Oswald probably would have allowed Arlo to die. But we needed Arlo's strength for the spell, so Oswald healed him. He remembers nearly dying by Chaos' minions' hands. Arlo has every right to be scared."

"I'm beginning to understand your claims about our demise as well." Felicia shifted uneasily. "Falcon, I can't guarantee my people will obey me and fight. They'd rather try to kill me or hide."

"Keeve, can you fetch Garrett?" Falcon stood and took Elias' hair in his hands and lifted the Howler's head from the table. "I'll take care of this."

Falcon slid away as Dad rose from his seat. Dad's strained smile didn't give me much confidence. He left without a word, leaving me, Felicia, and Cash alone. We didn't speak. No one had anything to say. Our path forward would be filled with fear and pain.

A soft, furry hellhound was placed in my lap. Her little red eyes opened and looked up at me. Would she survive this?

I'll protect you, Brina.

No, Joliet. I reached out and ran my fingers through her fur where she'd appeared beside me. *I need you to care for Victory. She needs you. She needs her mom.*

Very well. Fargo and my children will fight with you. Joliet took her pup and disappeared.

Beyond where Joliet had stood, Fargo and more hellhounds stood at the ready. They were massive. Would they be enough? Would any of us be enough? They would need to be. *We* would need to be.

Arlo walked into the room at the same time Falcon appeared at my side again. Each man took their seats. Dad and Garrett, the Howler, returned as Falcon took my hand. The bloody pool in the middle of the table remained a stark reminder of what would happen to us if we didn't work together to find a way to stop Chaos. But would the Darken fight?

"Garrett, thanks for coming," Falcon greeted the Howler who sat with a chair between himself and Arlo. Garrett didn't trust the Charmer. He didn't have reason to. This would be our first problem, a major hurdle. While all of us in the room, aside from Garrett, trusted each other to the extent enemies could, our people didn't have the excuse of being family and friends to fight beside each other.

"Keeve said Elias is dead." Garrett's eyes zeroed in on the blood. His nostrils flared at the scent.

"Yes, he is. Chaos killed him." Quickly, Falcon filled Garrett in on who Chaos was and what would become of everyone if Chaos was not stopped. "Your people no longer have a First Four leading them."

"There are six of us. I wouldn't necessarily say we have a 'people' anymore."

"Regardless, you spoke up for the other Howlers earlier. Congratulations, you've just earned yourself a death sentence as the First Four of the Howlers. Welcome to the meeting. It's time to discuss our plan."

Garrett gulped at Falcon's proclamation. He had to regret opening his mouth when he and his comrades entered the room. If I were him, I would be. My fear nearly made me regret being found by Falcon, but my heart ached at what I would have missed out on if he hadn't. My family. I would do anything to protect them now.

"We have little time." Falcon leaned his forearms on the edge of the table. He took everyone in. "As the Howlers discovered, Chaos isn't our only problem. His children are free as well, and they are plentiful. Keeve, you'll want to inform your other compounds so they are not taken unawares. Chaos also has a right-hand man. Well, woman. Her name is Wraith. She's his oldest child, spawned from his first villainy on this earth."

"Are his children as powerful as him?" Dad asked. "Can they appear and disappear as Chaos does?"

Arlo shook his head and spoke up before Falcon. "No, but that doesn't make them less dangerous. They roam in packs and cause havoc wherever they go. Similar to Shadows, their effects are mostly felt instead of seen."

Felicia wiped her hands over her face. "This really does seem hopeless."

I couldn't argue with her. How would we win a war against a monster who couldn't die? How could we beat back his children? Wouldn't more chaos just breed more of them?

"It *is* hopeless." Arlo slumped in his chair. "Rebuilding that wall is a waste of time. So is making a plan which will never work."

"Aren't you a ray of sunshine." I elbowed him in the side. Turning back to the others, I sat straighter. "If we sit here doubting we can win, we'll lose for sure. While I'm still adjusting to my identity as my memories return, I know one thing: we are the leaders of our people. If they perceive we feel hopeless, they will feel the same. If we portray confidence, they will fight harder."

"You're just giving them false hope," Arlo grumbled.

"Maybe," I relented. "It's worth a try. Either way, they'll be dead if we lose. Being filled with some hope can't hurt anyone instead of wallowing in despair until their end comes."

"You're right." Felicia sat up taller. "However, I echo my statement from earlier. Find someone else. I'll fill in for now, but I'm not strong enough to lead the Conjurers. We need to find someone who can out-power them, or someone who they respect."

"Understood." Falcon pointed at Garrett. "Will your people listen to you?"

"There's no one else. If there are more, I doubt we'll find them. They won't show their heads for a while, thinking Elias is still alive. The others will listen, but I'm not sure what they'll choose to do. I will do what I can."

"Good enough. Arlo, will your people listen to you?" Falcon asked his friend.

"They won't have a choice," Arlo answered, earning a groan from me. "What?"

I glowered at him. "You're grumpy, Arlo."

He rolled his eyes. "You are not only asking all the Darken and Phoenixes to fight against Chaos, and let's not forget about his children for even a second, but you're also asking all of us to work together. We are natural-born enemies, in case you forgot when you matured, Brina dear. The chances of us not killing each other before Chaos gets his hands on us is small. The

Phoenixes find the ways of the Darken deplorable. Especially those of Shadows and Charmers. My people still need sustenance, Brina. They need sex. And with humans, because we gain more strength from them. How do you expect them to gain strength when you cringe at what we do?"

My stomach soured. The Shadows had Falcon to keep them strong. Howlers ate meat, but there was plenty of that in the world, and Conjurers ate like humans. Arlo was right. The Charmers were a problem. They'd need to leave the compound to gain strength, and those unions weren't always consensual when the Charmer used their voice to persuade someone to do their will. How would the Phoenixes feel working with those they'd learned to hate? How would the Darken trust the Phoenixes not to kill them, especially after the Darken attacked the compound and killed so many Phoenixes?

"We have to try," I hedged.

"Try?"

"Yes, try, Arlo. If we don't try, we'll never know if it's possible. I can't say our people will love each other, but with a united enemy, maybe they'll put their differences aside to stay alive."

"That's a big maybe." Arlo glowered at me.

"Doesn't Adler prove Shadows and Charmers can work together? She's half of each."

Arlo scoffed. "Shadows and Charmers can put aside differences for quick roll in the hay. They'll probably try to kill each other when they're through."

"But you and Falcor are friends," I tried again.

Arlo's smile didn't light up his features with joy, but with evil mirth. "Your mate would have killed me without question before Chaos came into the picture. I'm sure Chaos not killing me disappointed him. Falcon took me under his wing for necessity's sake after we imprisoned that monster. I couldn't die, or Falcon would burn with the world. His past actions show how little our 'friendship' means to him, or have you forgotten all the lies he's told and the truths he's kept from me?"

"They were to protect—"

"Yes, Falcon," Arlo cut off his best friend, "they were to protect Brina, the mate you weren't supposed to have. And protect your people, the people who were supposed to be dead."

Awkward silence made Felicia squirm. The last thing we needed was infighting. But Arlo was right. How would everyone work together if we struggled right now? Was it even possible?

Voices, memories of conversations with Falcon, filled my mind. Everything still seemed so detached from the person I was before and the person I was now. My confusion about my identity didn't matter. I'd deal with that later.

"Arlo, stand up." I pushed my chair back and stood.

Arlo, the ever-charming Charmer, rolled his eyes as he liked to do to me, and stood. His eyes and mannerisms appeared bored. He stood about my height, so I didn't have to look up at him like I did Falcon and strain my neck.

"Take my hand." The command earned me another eyeroll and a puff of annoyance as Arlo took my outstretched hand. "Now, slide us anywhere."

Annoyance left Arlo's eyes and his brows rose a little as his eyes widened. "Anywhere? Why?"

"Just do it. Anywhere you want to go. Take us there."

His eyes narrowed as quickly as they'd grown in his shock. "What are you doing, Brina? Is this some sort of trap?"

"Arlo, you're much stronger than me, and I can guarantee you're more devious. Charmers may not fight, but I've been killed so many times I'm unsure how well I fight anymore. This isn't a trap. Slide."

He set his jaw in determination. Darkness overtook my vision. When I blinked, we stood on a knoll by the ocean. The saltiness of the air made me screw up my face. Arlo laughed.

"Not a fan of the sea?"

My eyes stared out into the dark depths as a memory of one of my deaths played again. "The last time I saw an ocean, I ran into the water as far as I could and ended up drowning. I knew

I'd be reborn, but that has never made death less traumatic." A shiver ran up my spine. "Falcon thinks my death after the birth of my sons was traumatic enough to wipe the memory from my mind. I wish I could remember more about the end of that life. I'd like to be free of other deaths I can remember so clearly."

Arlo watched me as I stared out into the darkness of night. He turned to the ocean after he'd finished his examination.

"Why did you drown yourself?"

"I was escaping Oswald. He'd found me. Wanted my blood. He was furious when he lost me to the water. It was dark like it is tonight. I liked to wander at night."

"Searching for Falcon."

"Falcon loves you, Arlo. He trusts you with not only his life, but mine. He didn't tell you things to protect you. He might have started your friendship with the goal of keeping you alive so Chaos wouldn't rule the world, but that's not why he's your friend now."

"If he really trusted me, he would have told me the truth. Yes, I wouldn't have been happy, but I would have…" Arlo's eyes misted. "I would have helped him look after your son. His son. The son he loves. Both of them. I would have protected both of them." Arlo cucked his head before raising it again, trying to control the emotions within him so he wouldn't tear up more. He'd consider crying a weakness. "He doesn't trust me, Brina. Not with the important things."

"You're wrong, Arlo. I can prove it."

He scoffed. "How?"

I shrugged and sat on the ground. After a few seconds of hesitation, Arlo joined me. He brought his knees up and loosely wrapped his arms around them. His curly hair rustled in the breeze coming off the ocean.

"What proof do you have?"

"I'm here with you." My answer didn't appease him. He glared over at me. "No, really, Arlo. Think about it. Chaos is running amok in the world. So are his so-called children whom we really need to discuss more. And yet, Falcon let you slide me anywhere in the world, as far from him as you wanted to go, without him. Yes, Falcon is probably trying to keep himself pulled together at the compound, but he trusted you to keep me safe. He could've stopped us, but he trusted you with the most important thing in his life. Falcon did what he thought was best for everyone. I didn't like being scared senseless when meeting him in this life, but there was a purpose greater than my happiness. I know the lies and secrets make Falcon seem untrustworthy, but you are probably the person Falcon trusts the most. You and Falcon, you're the last First Four we have, the strongest of us. I don't know if the Darken and Phoenixes can work together. I really don't. All I know is we have no chance of working as a team if you and Falcon are divided."

Arlo gave a slow nod, mulling over my words. I relaxed as he gave a heavy sigh. "I can't blame him for his secrets and doing what he thought was right." He opened and closed his mouth a few more times, as if he wanted to say something but didn't know how to say it.

"Spit it out, Arlo."

"I broke up with Adler."

I blinked. That had not been what I'd expected him to say. "When? Why? I thought you cared for her, or was that all an act?"

Irritation grew within me. Adler was my son Quest's sister. They were raised together. She and Quest were family, making Adler my family. No one, not even Arlo, would hurt my family and get away with it.

Arlo snorted yet again. I seemed to bring out the best in him. "Do you have any idea how terrified Falcon is right now? How much he regrets putting that mark on your face?" He indicated the Shadow mark Falcon had drawn into my face. I touched the raised mark as Arlo continued. "Chaos knows Falcon's greatest weakness now. He knows if he has you, or threatens you, Falcon will do whatever it takes to protect his mate. If anyone could stop Chaos, was strong enough to bring him down, it was Falcon. He was the only one of us Chaos feared. Now he has leverage on Falc."

Understanding went off like fireworks in my head. "And you don't want that to happen to Adler."

"If he found out about her..." Arlo rose and paced in the sand beside me. When he came to a stop, anger seemed to pour off him. He bent and then threw a rock out into the crashing waves. "I can't protect myself, Brina. How could I protect her?"

Falcon had said Charmers couldn't fight. Now that Arlo had brought up my position between Falcon and Chaos, I could understand why Arlo would sever ties with Adler. My gut told me Falcon would do the same if he'd had the choice.

Arlo placed both hands on his hips. "I wasn't nice. I hurt her. Told her I didn't care for her and used her so I could get you off my back about a girlfriend. Especially since Adler wouldn't sleep with me. In truth, that is something I admire about her. Any other woman would have offered herself up immediately once I began talking to them. Adler told me to go away because she wasn't interested in becoming a Charmer's dinner. She didn't believe me when I said I didn't have plans for that. She just... It's easy to be around her. She has a more loving, giving attitude than most Shadows and Charmers. She made me hope..." Arlo trailed off. His shoulders drooped with the weight of the world. "I can see why Falcon gave everything up for you, changed his entire life. I would do that for Adler."

His admission shocked me. Before I could respond, he kept going. "Since meeting Adler and growing closer to her, I haven't...my lust..." Arlo collapsed beside me. His wall came down—both physically and mentally–and I shuddered. The change had been so dramatic.

Arlo had appeared strong a moment ago. Now, his color had paled. His hair, usually a mousy brown color and silky smooth, had streaks of gray in it. The hair looked...malnourished? Lines appeared on his face, and Arlo seemed to be in pain. He'd lost a lot of weight. His clothes hung off him like he'd bought them a few sizes too big. He looked awful, like he'd aged fifty years in the blink of an eye.

"Arlo?" I reached out to him. He changed again before I could touch him.

"When a Charmer is as old as I am, they can portray an image of themselves to others without using their voice," he admitted.

"You're dying."

He shook his head. "I can't die from not feeding."

"Arlo... I... What are we going to do?"

"We?" Arlo smirked. "If *we* did anything, I wouldn't need to worry about Chaos killing me. I'd die by Falcon's hands."

My cheeks warmed. "You know that's not what I meant."

His smile faded. "Yes, but there's nothing to be done."

"Couldn't you just find...someone?"

"Brina, perfect Brina, did you just suggest I go make love to just anyone?"

I glowered at him. "You've done it before."

"Yes, but that way of life is no longer appealing. My heart belongs to Adler. If Oswald hadn't... If Chaos hadn't been loosed..."

He remained quiet and sat in the sand. My heart ached for him. He'd broken up with the woman of his dreams to save her while he withered away. Even before Chaos, Arlo had begun to lose his strength. Had he stopped feeding before we'd gone to the Shadows' underground caves? That was weeks ago!

"I won't be much use in a fight," Arlo admitted. "It's taking everything in me to keep my people in line."

"I understand. We have to try to fight, or we're dead anyway."

He nodded. "I'll fight for her. I'll die for her."

CHAPTER 4

Brina

A rlo stood and brushed the backside of his pants off. "Say nothing of this to anyone. Especially Adler. Like I said, I was cruel. She needs to believe I never cared for her. That's the only way I can protect her. When this is over, if we live, I hope she can forgive me."

"I'm sure she will once she understands."

"I was cruel."

"So you've said."

"She needed me. Her mom was killed in Oswald's attack." My heart broke for Adler. And for Quest. He'd thought of Adler's mom as his mom for so long. "I said some things I'll never be able to take back. The hurt on her face... The tears... Brina, so help me, if we live through this, I will never stop trying to win her affection again." Arlo's vow warmed my heart. That he was telling me all of this made me wrap my arms around him in a tight hug.

"Really?" Arlo scoffed but wrapped his arms around me.

Darkness engulfed us. In a blink, we appeared back in my dad's conference room.

"Dear Brina, thank you so much for that *enjoyable* conversation." Arlo leaned back and winked.

"Arlo." Falcon growled his friend's name. My mate's arm hooked around my waist, and I was dragged back into Falcon's hard chest. My toes curled as Falcon held me.

"Relax, Falc. Brina gave me something to think about." Arlo

33

sat in his chair and scooted closer to the table. "I don't hold out much hope that we'll beat Chaos. He'll exploit our weaknesses. He would love it if one of us turned on the others. Nothing would cause more mass panic. People fighting and running for their lives is just the ticket he's looking for. My people can't fight. It's not our way. However, we'll be willing to learn, willing to try."

"The same goes for my people," Garrett added. He ducked his head, but then raised it and continued. "We're small in number, but we're deadly."

Didn't I know that? I shivered. Falcon kissed the top of my head. If he could take those memories from me and put them on himself, he would. He blamed himself for my loss of life each time he came to my aid too late. But every time I died, I'd been at fault. I knew the rules, and I disobeyed them.

We will fight as well. Fargo came to stand between Falcon and Cash.

Falcon dug his fingers into his bonded hellhound's fur. "Fargo, take your sons to scout for Chaos' children. Find out what is happening to the humans. We need to know what condition the world is in."

We will go. Fargo and his sons disappeared.

"I also," Garrett hedged after the hounds had left, "know of a Conjurer who may be able to help us. Well, he can, but I'm not sure if he will."

"Why not? Who is he?" Arlo sat forward in his chair. "How do you, a Howler, know of this Conjurer?"

"A few years ago, he saved my life."

"Wait." Arlo held up his hands. "A *Conjurer* saved the life of a *Howler*?"

"I know. It doesn't seem real. However, this man is different. He's powerful. I'm not sure how he stayed out of Oswald's reach all this time. He would need to be strong and cunning."

"Do you know how to find this Conjurer?" Dad asked. My father sitting in a room filled with Darken, planning the demise of Chaos, still boggled my mind. The people in this room were natural enemies. If the leaders of the races didn't have knives to the other leader's throats, our people could learn to work together too, right?

"I know where we were when he found us. Whether he lived around there, I'm not sure. I think it's worth a try to find out." Garrett winced as he adjusted himself in his seat.

"Are you hurt?" I asked.

The Howler waved me off. "I'll heal fine. We don't have much time."

"I can get us there if you tell me an approximate location," Arlo offered. "However, depending on the time of day, Falcon may or may not be able to join us. If the sun is close to rising, we shouldn't chance his life, nor that of his people."

"The Phoenixes should remain as well." Dad nodded in agreement to Falcon's statement. "Felicia, you'll go with Garrett and Arlo."

I stood. "I'm going, too."

"Shadows rage, you will not." Falcon stood, glaring down at me. "We know nothing about this man, and you're a Phoenix."

"A Phoenix with a Shadow mark, Falcon. I'm an anomaly. Just like this Conjurer who should be dead. I'm proof Darken and Phoenixes can come to terms with their differences. We have to, or Chaos will tear us all apart." I hoped my eyes pleaded with Falcon as much as my words did. "Everyone has to be all in for this to work. We need to trust each other."

"I trust everyone here," Falcon countered. "I even trust the Howler's fear to keep him in line."

"Then trust me."

"I do trust you. That doesn't mean—"

"Falcon." Arlo stood. His movements and expression were solemn as he turned toward Falcon and me. "Brina, step aside please."

"Uh, sure?" I did as he'd asked. Arlo knelt in front of Falcon and bowed his head. What was he doing?

"Falcon Firestorm, First Four of the Shadows, first of the Darken, I, Arlo, First Four of the Charmers, give you my word that should your mate, Brina Firestorm, warrior Phoenix and Lady of the Shadows, come with us, I shall protect her with my life. Should I return without her, I forfeit my life. I will be her guardian and return her to you. This I vow."

I stood there, speechless, as Arlo gave his vow. It wasn't much in terms of words, but the room seemed to take on a heavier atmosphere, like air before a storm. Falcon's eyes glowed red, a sign of his high emotions.

"I accept your vow." Falcon's voice had deepened, and it even seemed to echo.

Arlo stood. When he began to remove his shirt, one button at a time, my heart began to pick up speed. Not because Arlo was hot and easy to look at, though that was the case—however my heart belonged fully to Falcon—but because I couldn't figure out what they were doing. Why was Arlo undressing at a time like this? Falcon had accepted the vow. Couldn't we leave now?

Falcon reached out, his eyes still glowing, and placed the tip of his index finger on the skin over Arlo's heart. With precision, Falcon began to draw something on Arlo's chest. I inched to the side for a better view. My eyes widened at the sight of Falcon's Shadow mark now arrayed on the Charmer's chest.

"Should you break your promise, Arlo, First Four of the Charmers, this mark will kill you. Should Brina die on your watch, you will not return to me." Falcon's eyes no longer glowed. They'd faded to their normal black, which most people found chilling. My muscles relaxed as Falcon's eyes dimmed.

Arlo's eyes swung over to me. "Lady Brina, I am Arlo, First Four of the Charmers."

"I know who you are—"

"Quiet," Falcon commanded softly. I closed my mouth, allowing Arlo to continue.

"It is my honor and privilege to guard you outside of these walls while your mate cannot accompany us. My life hangs in the balance, so please treat that with respect and do as I say. Do you accept my vow as your mate has?"

"Uh, yes?" Why in the world did he ask me that now and not before Falcon put the mark on him? I wanted to scream at them both for overreacting. I did not want to die, so therefore, I would make decisions which would not put me in harm's way on purpose. I'd learned that lesson a multitude of times...and yet I hadn't learned after the first time I'd died. Maybe they were right to give me a personal bodyguard.

Arlo gave a soft smile. "Don't do anything stupid, Brina."

Now it was my turn to roll my eyes. "It's not like I plan for things to happen. I didn't control my memories or Oswald's lunatic behavior."

Falcon let out a soft sigh and pulled something from his pocket. My brain recognized the black lace necklace with the red jewels.

"I'd hoped never to need to use this again." Falcon seemed ashamed by his actions.

"No, Falc. You're right. I'll feel better with it on." I turned, and Falcon fastened the necklace around my neck once more. Back when he'd tricked me into wearing the necklace, I'd felt collared like a dog, a prisoner of a monster. After Oswald tried to kill me, I'd never been so happy to wear the jewelry. With the necklace on, the spell encased in the jewels would allow Falcon to know my location. He could find me easily.

I turned to face Falcon. Arlo and Felicia had moved to stand by Garrett. In truth, I still feared the Howler, no matter that I'd matured. Howlers and I had too much bad blood between us for me to be comfortable with any of them yet. Wasn't that the problem facing us all?

"You look beautiful." Falcon reached up and touched the necklace. His fingers grazed my skin, sending electric tingles through me. "Be careful."

He bent down and pressed a firm kiss to my lips. Falcon pulled back sooner than I expected, giving away his concern for

MELANIE GILBERT

our situation even more. The Falcon facing down Oswald would have deepened the kiss until Arlo complained. This Falcon facing Chaos knew time was of the essence.

"I'll be careful," I promised.

"Stay by Arlo," Falcon added as I walked around the table to reach Arlo, Garrett, and Felicia. Cash stood just beyond the group, as helpless as Falcon was to protect his charge. Yeah, my gut told me he had it bad for her. As she glanced his way, I had a feeling the attraction was mutual.

Arlo held his hand out to me. Garrett held his other while Felicia clung to Garrett's arm. What did Felicia have to be so afraid of? The Conjurer wouldn't kill her, would he? Yeah, Felicia was in charge, but she didn't want to be. Surely the man we were heading to see knew Oswald had died. If he wanted to become First Four, he could step up to the plate. Felicia would be thrilled.

"Here we go." Arlo squeezed my hand and darkness encased us. When we'd finished sliding, we stood in a forest. Arlo blew out a breath. "We're lucky I could find a deep enough shadow close to the spot you met up with this Conjurer. The sun is rising. We made the right choice in not bringing the Shadows."

My stomach turned sour. Up until now, I'd trusted the people around me to keep me safe. Yes, I trusted Arlo, but as he'd made perfectly clear, he couldn't fight. Felicia could use magic, and she'd always been kind to me. Garrett, I had no reason to trust him. Though, Falcon said he trusted Garrett's fear. The Howler wouldn't jeopardize his life by betraying us. Falcon would tear him apart, and Garrett knew it. Plus, Garrett feared Chaos.

I missed Falcon at my side. That was the problem. Of everyone in the world, I trusted my life to him the most. He would fight for me because he'd had centuries without me. I trusted Falcon's desperation.

"You were right," Arlo turned and whispered in my ear as he pretended to take in our surroundings. "About Falcon. I was wrong to doubt him."

38

"You're the closest thing he has to a brother. He loves you." I, too, kept my voice low.

Arlo nodded as Garrett called to us. "It's over here."

Garrett led the way through the forest. Felicia dropped back to walk near Arlo and me. Garrett didn't seem bothered by the space left between us as he searched the area.

"Anyone feel like searching for a powerful Conjurer might be a trap?" Felicia muttered low enough that Garrett's Howler hearing wouldn't pick up her voice.

"If it is," Arlo answered, "keep your magic ready."

"And what's it going to do against another Conjurer? Especially one powerful enough to evade Oswald for years. We should have brought more backup."

"What? More Phoenixes?" Arlo hissed. "Charmers wouldn't do the trick, and the Conjurers can't be trusted as far as you can throw them. Which, for your size, isn't far. We should have brought Orion."

I smacked Arlo on the arm. "We were not bringing my son here. I put my foot down." What was Arlo even thinking?

Felicia grunted in agreement. "We could have waited until night. Then the Shadows could have come."

"That's a lot of wasted time," I disagreed, nearly tripping over a branch.

Arlo rolled his eyes as he helped steady me. "Falcon's wrath, you're going to be the death of me. Literally."

I scowled at him. He ignored my expression and grabbed my upper arm to tow me along behind him. Yes, his life depended on me staying alive, but I wasn't a child. However, since his life hung in the balance, I kept my retort to myself. In the grand scheme of things, this wasn't worth an argument over.

We scanned the forest for danger as we continued to follow Garrett. Part of me agreed with Felicia about waiting until night to do this. Another part screamed we worked on a time limit, though what that limit was, I didn't know. Whenever Chaos got bored and wanted his answer? He had to know we wouldn't work with him. Didn't he expect us to rebel and fight him? Maybe he wanted us to. A war would bring more chaos into the world. And if there was infighting, that would certainly strengthen him.

"Here. This is where I nearly died." Garrett lifted his nose into the air. "Air is clean. No one has been here in a while."

Arlo sighed and his hand loosened on my arm, though it didn't drop away. It hadn't missed my attention that he'd awkwardly positioned him and me in the darkest shadow given off by a tree, though I wasn't sure the shadow was dark enough for us to slide. Maybe being in the shadow gave Arlo some sense of security. He was a Charmer, and they tended to flee a fight instead of head into it. And he knew more about the deepness of a shadow needed to slide.

"So, now what?" Arlo ran his free hand through his curly hair, growling softly in his chest when his fingers caught a knot. "We've wasted our time."

"We haven't even searched yet." Felicia glared at Arlo.

"I'll scout the area, see what I can smell," Garrett offered. He'd directed the statement to me.

Arlo and Felicia turned to me as well, just as Garrett had. I blinked at them all. What? Were they waiting for *my* permission?

"I'm not in charge of this adventure," I clarified. "Arlo's the powerful First Four. Felicia is a new First Four along with Garrett. I'm nothing. The rest of you are something."

"You're Lady of the Shadows," Arlo countered. "You are here in Falcon's stead, making you in charge."

"No one said that before we left! I would have argued the point! You can't just spring that on me now. It's not fair."

"Arguing the point doesn't change anything. You're still in charge. Now, hurry up and decide if that's what should be done." Arlo's eyes scanned the forest again. "Chaos isn't the only being to fear. His children will track us down soon. Especially if we have discord between us. Keep the peace everyone. Our lives depend on it."

"Lovely." I wiped my hands over my face, feeling the bumps of my Shadow mark. What would Falcon do? He would take the chance of trusting Garrett to protect me and our family. But Garrett was a Howler, the most vicious of all the Darken. Capable of tearing all three of us apart before we could slide away.

My hands turned sweaty at the thought. I wiped them on my pants and cleared my throat. Hundreds of years ago, I wouldn't have blinked an eye at this situation. Garrett wouldn't have put the fear of death in me. I'd even hunted down Falcon, the worst of them all. Many of the Darken died by my hands. I'd been a Phoenix warrior with a reputation similar to my father's.

Now I stood there shaking at the idea of Garrett turning into his animalistic form and tearing me apart. It wasn't Garrett's fault. He was too young to be any of my killers. The Phoenix part of me could decipher that much about him, though I didn't know how. Even Dad didn't. The creator kept some of his secrets to himself.

Logic finally cried out louder than my fear. We'd followed Garrett this far. Why stop now?

"Lead the way. We're not separating." I stepped forward and pulled Arlo with me.

"I'll need to change forms to have a greater sense of smell." Garrett cringed, his sharp canines showing. "I will not attack you."

Arlo took my hand, portraying the role of my protector, but his squeeze let me know he'd also be my support. I wasn't sure how much Falcon had told him about my life, and he'd heard some of it from me, but Falcon wasn't the only person Arlo cared for. Even if he was a pain in my backside. Arlo did like me. And I liked Arlo. I didn't have a brother. If I did, I'd want one like Arlo.

Garrett's body began to change. He fell forward on legs which were now jointed differently, like a wolf's, and his nose and mouth narrowed into something similar to a snout. More hair sprung out of his skin to cover nearly all of his body. His clothes remained on him, but stretched to their max. His teeth grew longer, more pointed, and saliva dripped from his mouth. Garrett was every bit the monster I remembered from my nightmares.

The Howler lifted his nose into the air. He either found what he wanted or didn't find what he'd hoped. Either way, he gave a low growl and prowled deeper into the woods.

"Here we go." Arlo kept my hand and followed after Garrett. Felicia followed behind us. Maybe we should have put her up front in case Garrett attacked, she being the Conjurer and most likely to stop an attack quickly, but apparently I was in charge, so I led the way, preceded by my sworn protector.

Time passed and Garrett searched, backtracking to find a scent trail in the area. Maybe we were wrong? Maybe the Conjurer was just passing through and wasn't anywhere around here? How long ago did this event happen?

"Well, what have we here?"

We spun, and my heart stalled. Red hair and glowing hands. Oswald!

CHAPTER 5

Brina

Fear froze me in place until my brain caught up with my eyes. The man wasn't Oswald, though he did have similar red hair with streaks of blond. He stood taller than Oswald had, and his features made him attractive whereas Oswald had been, well, ugly.

Garrett shifted back to being human-looking. "This is him."

"Yes, this is me." The Conjurer smirked. "Now, what brings such a diverse bunch to my doorstep? I should kill you all for finding my location, but you've intrigued me. Especially the Phoenix with a Shadow mark holding the hand of the First Four Charmer."

Arlo nudged me forward, pushing the small of my back. No one said I had to do the talking when we found him! Sure, I'd made the decision to follow Garrett, but I didn't know I'd be introducing us. If I'd known, I would have started working on my speech instead of winging this.

I cleared my throat, buying myself time. "My name is Brina, Brina Firestorm. Falcon, First Four of the Shadows, is my mate."

"So, you're Brina." The Conjurer took me in from toes to head. Even though his eyes weren't filled with lust, they were calculating in their examination. I tried to keep my head up. How had I been a kick-butt Phoenix before and now I struggled to keep eye contact with a random Conjurer?

"Yes, I'm Brina." I tilted my chin up a little more. "You've heard of me?"

"Oh yes." The man's eyes gleamed as his smirk turned wolfish. "My father talked about you all the time, Mother."

"Moth...what?" I shook my head. I'd remember if I had three kids, right? And as a Phoenix, I'd never sleep with anyone other than my mate, and if I'd had a mate prior to Falcon, then Falcon and I couldn't have bonded. A second bonding was impossible. Was I missing more memories than I thought?

"Mother," he repeated. "For all intents and purposes, you are my female given DNA."

"It's a good thing Falcon didn't come with us," Arlo muttered. Louder, he addressed the man. "'For all intents and purposes' isn't going to fly. Start at the beginning. Your father, who is he?"

"Oswald, First Four of the Conjurers, and a nightmare of a man."

"I never slept with Oswald," I blurted out.

"No, you didn't," the mysterious man agreed. "Still, you are my mother. Now, what brings you here, Mother?"

"Stop calling her that," Arlo growled out. "What's your name?"

"Cassius."

"Well, Cassius, why don't you stick your—"

"Arlo!" I punched him in the arm. "You're not helping. Let him explain before you tell him to put a piece of anatomy somewhere it shouldn't go."

"Brina." Cassius had lost his humored smirk. "Why are you here? Why come find me? Why trust a Howler to bring you here? The Darken don't get along with each other, let alone with a Phoenix."

"Oswald is dead." This surprised Cassius. He raised his eyebrows. I continued the explanation, "He used most of the Darken to fight against the Phoenixes. It was my fault. He wanted me."

"He always did. He craved you."

Um, gross and a lot uncomfortable. If Oswald wasn't already dead, I would have sent Falcon to kill him just for his creepiness.

"Falcon and I killed him, but Oswald's death led us to an even worse problem."

"Worse than Oswald? How can such a thing be?" Cassius was back to his amused, sarcastic nature.

I turned to Arlo and tipped my head to Cassius. "It's your story. Fill him in."

"Fine." Arlo pushed me over to a large boulder near us. "Sit."

"I'm not a dog."

"Sit."

"Fine."

Arlo sat beside me with his hand in mine. He'd put us in a deeper shadow by sitting us on the boulder. Always thinking of an exit, that man. I needed to stop fighting him.

"Oswald's death," Arlo began, "opened the way for a dark creature to escape a prison the First Four put him in. His name is Chaos and he plans to destroy the world, starting with the rest of the First Four and prominent leaders of the races. Including the Phoenixes."

"That will be tough, no?" Cassius crossed his arms and studied Arlo.

"No, it won't. He's already killed Elias and all but a handful of Howlers. Garrett and those Howlers were lucky to survive. He destroyed one race of Darken in minutes."

"Interesting. And you came to me because?"

"The Darker and Phoenixes need to work together if we have any hope of defeating Chaos," I answered.

"Though, it sounds to me as if he's powerful enough to overthrow you all."

Arlo tightened his hold on my hand. In his irritation, he probably didn't know he did.

"And once he overthrows us, how long do you think it will take him to track you down? You'll be the next most powerful being to destroy. Then, he'll move on to the rest of the world."

Cassius nodded as he mulled Arlo's words around in his head. "And you came to me for my help."

"You've remained hidden from Oswald for quite some time," Felicia answered Cassius' unasked question.

"And you are?"

"Felicia, new First Four of the Conjurers. That's Garrett, new First Four of the Howlers."

Cassius smirked at Garrett. "Yes, I remember him. Not his name, but had I known he'd bring you here, I might have enjoyed watching him die."

Garrett gulped. He'd need to grow a stronger backbone to lead his people. Even if he felt fear, he couldn't show it. But Garrett was young. Too bad he didn't have time to grow into his role.

"We can even offer you the position as First Four of the Conjurers," Felicia proposed.

Cassius scoffed. "I am a son of Oswald, a hated leader. No one will follow me."

"They don't want to follow me, either."

"Alright." Arlo stood and pulled me to my feet. "Are you coming with us, or are you going to let the world burn and die along with it?"

Cassius gave his classic smirk. "Well, when you put it that way, it sounds like I don't have a choice."

"You do. They're both not good choices." Arlo returned Cassius' smirk. "Besides, I can't wait to see Falcon's face when you explain how Brina is your mother. I bet he's going to love that."

"Well let's not keep my stepfather waiting. I assume you'll slide us to his location, Charmer?" If Cassius feared Falcon, or anyone at all, he didn't show it. He walked over to Arlo and held out his hand. "I've never slid before, but I know the basics."

"It can be disorienting the first time," I said as Felicia took my hand. Garrett hesitantly grasped Cassius' hand while the Conjurer's other hand took Arlo's.

"I'm sure I'll be fine, Mother, but thank you for your concern." The smile Cassius turned on me startled me before Arlo slid us to the conference room. His eyes held sincerity, not his usual dark humor.

Falcon, Dad, and Cash stood together in the darkest corner of the conference room. Cash needed darkness, though the other two didn't. Considering they were talking, standing together allowed them not to yell across the room. They were kind to think of Cash's comfort.

"You found him." Dad walked to his seat across the table from us and put his hands on the back of his chair. He smiled at Cassius. "Welcome. I am Keeve Firestorm."

"Ah, that makes you my grandfather." Of course Cassius had to lead with that. Did he want to die now?

"What?" Falcon appeared at my side. "What is he talking about?"

"We're wondering the same." Arlo released my hand and waved at our new ally. "This is the Conjurer who saved Garrett. His name is Cassius, and he's already a pain in the butt to work with."

Arlo flopped down into his chair, more grumpy than normal. Breaking up with Adler and struggling to keep his strength up didn't help his attitude. If there had been anyone else to help us slide to Cassius, I would have left Arlo here instead of sliding and using his strength. His actual form, not the one he conveyed to others, worried me.

"Let's sit down then, and Cassius can introduce himself." Dad waved Cassius to a chair near him. This time, Garrett sat beside Arlo to keep more distance between him and our guest. How the dynamics had changed so quickly.

"What do you wish to know?" Cassius asked when we had all taken our seats.

"How did you evade Oswald for so long, and how is Keeve your grandfather?" Falcon led the questioning. "Raven and

Brina are both mated, and Athena has no mate. Phoenixes mate for life, and Raven's mate Cove isn't a Conjurer."

"Ah, yes." Cassius sat forward and leaned on the table with his forearms. "Those questions actually go hand-in-hand. To answer the first, I shall start by answering the second."

"Either way."

"Keeve is my grandfather, because Brina is my mother. More or less." Again, I couldn't figure out how I would be his mother.

Falcon glanced down at me. I held up my hands.

"I don't know what he's talking about. In my past lives, I've only been pregnant once." Even with missing memories, I was sure I hadn't had a Conjurer's baby.

Dad turned in his chair to face Cassius. "What does 'more or less' mean?"

Cassius wove his fingers together on the table as he answered. "It's not a secret that Oswald did experiments on his people."

"Yes, we all know that." Falcon's impatience created a small growl in his voice. I placed my hand on his thigh to calm him. Thankfully, for everyone's sake, my touch worked. No one needed a jealous Falcon killing Cassius before we had answers.

"Continue." Dad waved Cassius on.

"I'm not sure what his experiments consisted of before my birth. Chances are, they weren't very pretty. However, after my birth, he focused on duplicating me, my birth, my genetics."

"Because you're stronger than you should be for your age," Felicia guessed.

"Yes. Oswald had experimented on my mother, my biological mother. He was always very open with me since my youth about his plans. He never expected me to flee. Oswald wanted me to help him with his goal, but even as a Darken, I couldn't stomach the things he did."

"If your mother was a Darken, not a Phoenix, how is Brina your mother?" Arlo rubbed circles into his temples, trying to tie things together.

"I'm getting there."

"Go faster or, hellhounds wrath, I will break it out of you," Falcon threatened.

Cassius narrowed his eyes at Falcon. His jaw tightened. "You are a Shadow, the first and the strongest of your kind, but you are still susceptible to magic. Do not threaten me."

Many eyebrows rose at Cassius' audacity to speak so freely to Falcon, returning threat for threat. I tightened my grip on Falcon's leg just in case Cassius had tipped the scale of Falcon's patience.

"To resume my explanation," Cassius continued to glare at my mate, "Oswald did experiments. For the experiment I was the result of, he forced himself on my mother, impregnated her, and somehow used the magic from a golden Phoenix feather belonging to Brina to enhance the pregnancy. Thus, Brina's DNA is as much a part of me as my biological mother's and father's are."

Blood drained from my face. How had Oswald gained access to one of my feathers? How had he used it to create Cassius? What else had he done with the feather?

Cassius continued before I could come to grips with his shocking revelation. "Once Oswald discovered how much stronger I was than other Conjurers at such a young age, he devised a plan to gain access to more of Brina's DNA. He trapped Falcon and Brina in a small house, blocking their ability to slide away. The plan was to separate Falcon from Brina and steal her away. Alas, when he arrived, Brina was dead. He tried to use her ashes on another woman he'd impregnated, but the experiment didn't work. In his rage, he killed both mother and child."

I closed my eyes at the horror of what Cassius described. I'd known Oswald had a crazy streak and sought after power. The Darken were evil, I knew that, but hearing about the atrocities still made me want to gag.

Arlo leaned back in his chair, lifting the front two legs off the ground. "That's why he attacked Brina in her past lives, and why he tried to kill her in this life while taking her blood. But why would he try to kill her?"

"I don't know," Cassius admitted. "I'd already left him by then. Brina's DNA gave me more power than any other Conjurer ten times my age, more than any Conjurer alive, by the time I was eight years old. Oswald forced me to participate in his experiments. When he commanded me to force myself on a woman he'd chosen to see if our child would be strong like me, I left. I'm not a saint, but I would not allow that man to use or kill my child.

"I never knew my mother. Oswald killed her after she'd delivered me. A fact he regretted after his second experiment with Brina's ashes failed because he considered my mother to be a better vessel. But my mother was dead, and I never knew her. Therefore, with Brina's DNA inside me, she is my mother."

Arlo dropped his chair to the ground. "That's not how motherhood works."

"I'll be your mom." Everyone looked at me in shock. I'd even surprised myself. The words just slipped out as my heart broke for Cassius.

"Brina?" Falcon put his hand over mine on his leg.

"I'll be your mom, Cassius," I repeated. He, too, looked at me with surprise written across his face. Even though he'd claimed me as his mom, he'd never expected me to accept that role in his life. "Everyone deserves to have a family who loves them. You had a nightmare of a childhood. No one was there to protect you from Oswald and his evil. Well, Falcon and I will be here for you now."

"You're sure?" Cassius hedged, as if he didn't believe my offer.

To tell him the truth, taking him on as a child scared me. I didn't yet know if I trusted him as fully as I should. To be his mom, I'd need to put all my trust in him, but he was part Oswald. And yet, if he'd been secretly working for Oswald, wouldn't he have been at the battle, saved Oswald's life even? Oswald had hurt so many people. Cassius didn't deserve to be alone anymore just because of who his father had been. How long had he been alone?

"We're sure." Falcon wove his fingers through mine. My head whipped over to stare into my mate's dark eyes. Falcon nodded to me. That he'd given in so quickly shocked me as much as my own outburst had.

Turning back to Cassius, I gave him my warmest smile, trying to put him at ease. My own heart pounded harder than it had before. I could end up regretting this decision. Or, taking Cassius on as my child would be one of the best decisions I'd ever made. Only time would tell. "I have sons who are a mix of Shadow and Phoenix. Why not add Phoenix and Conjurer to the list?"

"Thank you, Brina, Falcon." Cassius nodded his head as he addressed us.

"Now that the heritage of our new Conjurer friend is taken care of, how do we stop Chaos?" Arlo crossed a leg over the other.

The silence in the room was deafening and unencouraging. How could we kill a being who couldn't be killed? How could we trap him when he was too strong and we were too weak? The First Four had only been able to trap him before because they had worked together for the first, and last, time.

"We work together." My idea was met by deadpan faces. What? I thought it was a good idea.

"I thought we'd already decided on that. But what do we do after we work together?" Arlo refrained from giving me an eyeroll. He probably didn't have the strength for that. I needed to talk with Falcon about his friend's physical limitations soon.

"I don't know," I admitted, "but the First Four worked together last time. We can do it this time."

"Isn't that why we're here making a plan?"

"Arlo, think about it. Your people can't fight. No offense, but you guys are useless right now."

"None taken. Continue."

"The Conjurers have their magic. They can't teach that to anyone, *but* if we knew more about what they can do, we could figure out how to use magical abilities to help in battle. Phoenixes spar and train all the time. They can train the Charmers in basic hand-to-hand combat. The Howlers have the weakness of numbers, but their teeth and claws are a great asset. Trust me, I know this. The Charmer's voices, do they have an effect on Chaos' children? We need to focus on keeping the world, the humans, safe while trying to take down Chaos. Yes, Arlo? Why are you shaking your head?"

"No offense, Brina, but protecting humans doesn't seem to be a top priority at the moment. I get Phoenixes protect humans, but we have bigger problems. It just doesn't seem like an important priority."

"Maybe not, but Chaos draws strength from them, and after the Charmers have used humans for their pleasures for almost as long as this world is old, you owe it to them to help keep them safe, Arlo. The Shadows owe them, too, for making them afraid. Howlers have used them as food. Again, humans are owed. Conjurers have tormented and tortured them for ages. If any of you wish to deny the charges against you, please speak up, or shut your mouths and start repenting of your sins. They've brought us to this point."

When no one spoke up to deny my accusations, I continued. "We've decided to work together, but we don't know how that will happen. Our people don't know how to work together. They don't trust each other. How can they go to battle when they can't trust the person standing next to them? They can't. They'll all die because they're too busy watching their back so an ally doesn't stab them in the back. Literally."

"What do you suggest?" Dad leaned back in his chair. His eyes sparkled with pride. Oh crap, even he considered me in charge of this venture. And I really had no plan beyond this. I should've kept my mouth shut. I hadn't learned my lesson from Garrett speaking up for the Howlers only to find himself their leader.

I glanced up at Falcon. He gave me a slow nod. A smile tugged at his lips, but he wouldn't let it develop more than that. He should be leading this, not me. Any of them should. I'd died over and over and over. Did none of them remember that? I made bad decisions, and those decisions had gotten me killed. A lot. If I made bad decisions now, I could be responsible for thousands of deaths, or even the end of the world.

That thought alone froze my mind. The entire population of Earth depended on me. Well, unless my ideas were vetoed, but if they weren't, everyone could die.

"Brina." Falcon used his fingers beneath my chin to turn my face to him. "You were once a fierce warrior, one so brave and valiant she faced me without fear."

"I have more to lose now."

"I know, but you also have more to fight for. You have a family to fight for. Children. Whatever decision you make, you'll do it with your family in mind." Falcon leaned in and pressed a soft kiss to my lips.

"Why does it have to be me?" I groaned when he pulled back.

"Because you are the only person people will trust," Arlo surprised me by speaking up. "If any of the First Four, especially me and Falcon, or Keeve speak up, people will believe we have our own interest at heart. You belong to the Phoenixes, but also to the Darken. Your children are Phoenix and Darken. You'll protect them. People will respect you for accepting Cassius into your family without question. Not that that's why she did so," Arlo assured my newest son who nodded in understanding.

"All you need to do is think of a first step." Falcon ran a hand through my hair. "What should we do right now? You say we need to work together. How should we start?"

I rose and began to pace, thinking out loud. "We're on a time constraint. There's no time to train everyone to work with everyone else. The Shadows have returned home because of the sun. If we could introduce at least one race to another…"

I bit my lower lip. An idea presented itself as I walked along the wall of Dad's conference room. It could work, but it was also risky. But Chaos could attack at any time, or return to hear our answer about working with him or not. Then there were his minions, his children as he called them. And this Wraith person Falcon had mentioned, Chaos' first child. They destroyed the earth and its people at this very moment.

"Okay, here's what we'll do." I leaned on the back of my chair. "We'll create three to six small groups. In each group, we'll have at least one person from each race. There are fewer Howlers. If they feel safer having a buddy in the group, that will be fine. That's why the number of groups isn't set." Garrett nodded his understanding. "These groups will spend every minute together. They'll eat together, sleep together, and train together. Their goal is to learn about the other races and use that information to figure out how to work together. The Phoenixes can help the Charmers learn to fight, but that's risky for how many people there will be. We could also break them down into smaller groups. However, the mixed groups will lead the larger army in divisions. The races will be mixed together then. So we need to have the Conjurers and Shadows find a way to work together. We'll change things as we go along, but we need to assemble these mixed groups together."

"Assign the groups," Dad ordered. "If you need help deciding who should be in them, talk to their leader. Arlo and I will work together to arrange training for his people. I assume Falcon and Felicia will do the same for theirs." The two nodded. "If there are any issues with a member of our race, we will take care of the situation. Disagreements will not be allowed. Those only empower our enemy. Do whatever you need to do to keep peace amongst our peoples."

The others nodded in agreement. Each seemed on board with what we needed to do. I prayed this was the right path. As I looked around the room, no one objected to the plan. I almost wished someone would vote against my plan so I'd be off the hook and no one would die because of me.

When no one spoke up, I blew out a deep breath. "Okay then, let's hope this works."

CHAPTER
6

Brina

"Honestly, everyone I used to know is dead." Felicia and I hurried through the hallways of the Phoenix compound with Cash behind us, watching our backs. The Conjurer nearly jogged to keep up with me. "I can't advise you about which Conjurers to pick for your teams."

"Maybe I can be of some help." Cassius ran up behind us. "If the people I used to know are still alive, they may join us."

"Cash, take Felicia and Cassius to wherever the Conjurers are. Felicia, I don't care what you have to do, get your people on board. Cassius, help her."

"Yes, Mom."

I smiled over at the redhead. He gave me a small, shy smile back. For as pompous as he had been, the thought of family had evened out his temperament. For now. He needed his arrogance back to outshine the other Conjurers.

"You sound like a true leader." Felicia winked at me. Cash had them away before I could retort. Dad had ordered most of the lights in the hallways be removed so our allies could come and go as needed, along with not weakening the Shadows.

Turning, I again sped down the hallway. The people I needed to see worked outside in the courtyard cleaning up after the battle with Oswald. So much had changed in twelve hours. I almost wished Oswald hadn't been killed. At least with him, we knew what we were up against. Chaos was...well, chaotic. We didn't know anything, and that was beginning to mess with my mind. Chaos probably wanted, probably even planned, his moves for these results. The more mystery he created, the more we would fear and act on that fear. People who feared made rash, illogical decisions. If given too much time, we'd go crazy.

Phoenixes walked the hallways on missions to retrieve supplies or food for those Phoenixes still working. Each nodded as they passed by. None would look me in the eyes. I'd been taunted when I returned here. I'd warned them about Oswald. No one but my family and close friends had listened. How the mighty had fallen.

Outside, the sun shone down from high overhead. The wall didn't look much improved. The debris from it imploding had been mostly cleared up.

"Where's the debris?" I waved at the ground around the wall as I approached Azar.

"Hey, Bri." Azar wrapped me up in a tight hug. "You did amazing. I'm so proud of you." He pulled back to look at me. "You have an amazing family. I'm happy for you."

"I just want to keep them all alive. Now, debris."

"Right." Azar turned to examine the wall with me. "The Shadows were key to removing the large boulders and piles of rock. They would slide them away. Came in handy. I think their help improved the Phoenix's opinions on Shadows."

"We could use everyone working together. In fact, that's why I need to talk with you, Raven, Orion, and Serenity. We're in much more trouble than we were before."

Azar nodded, turning serious quickly. "Rumors are flying around saying that. No one knows what's happening."

"Dad will be briefing everyone, but I need to brief the four of you, because I need your help specifically."

"Anything I can do to help, I will."

"I hoped you'd say that. Just know this might get you killed."

Azar shrugged. "It's happened before."

"Yeah, but before, there wasn't a chance of the world being destroyed before you were reborn."

Azar paled. "That bad?"

"Worse."

"Okay. What do you need from me?"

"Find Raven and Serenity. I'll grab Orion. Meet in Dad's office."

Azar turned without a word and strode to the other side of the courtyard. My sister and friend worked over there with their mates. I hoped their men wouldn't hate me when this was all said and done, but the women were better warriors than the males, and the men knew it.

Faces I knew stood out against those I didn't as I scanned the crowd for my son. Names popped into my mind as I recognized Phoenixes. Sometimes a memory would quickly play. I didn't dwell on them. If we lived through this, I'd reexamine those memories. For now, they didn't matter. If we died soon, I wouldn't need to remember anything.

Orion hefted a large rock up onto his shoulder. Wow, he was strong. Why had they not put him in the field? Oh, right, they made fun of him instead because of his dark hair and lack of wings. Irritation and anger welled up inside me at the unfairness of it all. I'd fixed things for Orion, though maybe not as much as I wanted. He still worked alone while others lifted large rocks in pairs. Time. Time would solve our issues. If we had enough time before we all died.

Shaking the hopeless thoughts from my mind, I walked across the courtyard. Orion saw me coming and dropped his rock to the ground.

"You're alright?" He scanned my face. "You're pale."

"I'm scared. However, that can't be helped right now. Come with me to Dad's office. Azar, Ren, and Raven are meeting us there."

"Okay, let's go."

Together, Orion and I walked back into the building. Halfway to Dad's office, Falcon appeared at my side. My fear had called him. I hadn't lied to Orion. I'd been nervous until I'd reached his side. Now, the fear of losing my family and close friends who were pretty much family, scared me to death.

"I'm sorry, darling." Falcon took my hand as we continued to walk. "Had I seen the future, known what a toll my decisions would have on those I loved centuries later, I would have found another way to destroy this monster."

"There was no way you could have predicted anything like this future for yourself."

"No. At the time, I loved nothing except myself. Now, I too have much to lose." Falcon peered over my head at Orion on my other side. "How I wish to hide you and your brother away, but such a decision is futile."

"I want to help." Orion held his head higher. "I've never been allowed to fight against evil. If everyone else I love is fighting, so will I. I'm not afraid to die. I'm only afraid to lose people while I have my hands tied behind my back being useless like I've been my entire life. Give me this chance."

"You'll have your chance," I promised him. "Just be careful."

"I said I'm not afraid to die, Mom. I didn't say I wanted to die." Orion winked at me, a small smile playing on his lips. My heart warmed. I really did like being called Mom.

Azar, Raven, and Serenity arrived not long after Orion and I reached Dad's office. Falcon hated to excuse himself, but he needed to ready his Shadows for war. Hawke couldn't run things by himself this time. Orion had ducked his head when Falcon gave me a dizzying, passionate kiss.

"Raven filled me in about Chaos." Azar didn't wait for the door to even close before he began the conversation. "How do we stop him?"

"I don't know." I hated to admit such a thing, but they needed to know the truth. In my plan, they were sticking their necks out more than the rest of the Phoenixes. And this plan wasn't really a plan yet. It was an idea of a plan. "I have a start to a plan. It might even be a pointless start, but it's something."

"What do we do?" Ren crossed her arms and leaned against

Dad's desk. My friend was a Commander among the Phoenixes. She and I had been rivals while growing up. Now, Serenity was a good friend. She'd helped Falcon protect our children.

"I've created four teams. Each team will have one, or in the case of the Howlers, two, representatives from each race. Each of you, Orion, Azar, Raven, and Serenity, are the Phoenix representatives on your team if you agree to fill the position."

"You want me?" Orion's eyes couldn't grow bigger. "I've never been on a mission before. I've never seen battle before, aside from last night."

"You have special traits that give you more of an edge than the average Phoenix. You can slide, you have better night vision. And you're loyal to me, and I trust you. I can't say the same for a lot of people here."

"I'll do it." Raven hugged me tight. "You are brilliant, little sister. Keep telling yourself that. Don't tear yourself down, or you'll begin to believe the lies."

"I don't want to be the reason we all die." My arms tightened around Raven. How I'd missed her. Well, I would have missed her more if I'd remembered her in my past couple lives.

Raven pulled back and looked me square in the eyes. "Believe in yourself. We all believe in you."

"This is probably a stupid idea," I reiterated.

Ren groaned. "The First Four trapped Chaos last time, just the four of them. Now, all of the Darken, and the Phoenixes who were not there last time, are combining forces to go up against him. We can do this. Yes, people will die, but for the greater good, we can do this."

"We just need to do it in time," Azar added. "Where are the rest of our teams? There's no better time to get started than the present."

Tears stung my eyes. "Thanks. All of you, thank you."

"Enough with the sentiments. Let's go." Ren marched to the door. "Where are we meeting everyone?"

"Orion, you'll meet your team in the conference room next

door. Quest will be your Shadow representative. I want you and your brother to play around with your mixed heritage. Find out what each of you can do that you didn't know before, back when you thought you were only Phoenix and only Shadow." Orion nodded, his demeanor determined. "You'll also have a Howler named Ronan and a Charmer named Ainsley. Your Conjurer will be Cassius, your brother."

Orion blinked. "I have another brother? You and Falcon—"

"It's a long story. Due to an experiment by Oswald, Cassius has some of my Phoenix DNA. He has no family, so he'll be part of ours."

"You trust him that much?"

"Yes, Orion. Your father does, too. He's been as lonely as you and Quest. I think he's a good fit for us." I still prayed we'd made the right decision. Trust in family was key, but trusting a Darken was hard. Especially a Conjurer. However, I would give Cassius what trust I could.

Orion gave a small smile. "Okay then. I'll go meet with my brothers and we'll see if Cassius has any of your traits we can use against Chaos."

"Good luck. Please, *please*, be careful."

Orion leaned in and kissed my forehead. "I'll do my best."

My heart constricted and breathing became difficult as Orion closed the door behind him. He could have slid next door, but sliding wasn't his first instinct like it was for Quest.

"Breathe, Bri." Azar squeezed my shoulder. "Both of your boys, err, all of your boys, have good heads on their shoulders. I assume this Cassius does anyway."

"He hid from Oswald for hundreds of years."

"In that case, he has a very good head on his shoulders. Give them a chance. Now, who am I with?"

Lifting the paper, I read off the names. "You're with Astrid. Azar, you have to keep her safe."

"I'll do my best. You know I will."

"I know. The others are Jasper, a Howler, and Arlo suggested

Laura for your Charmer. Felicia and Cassius are still working on giving me a Conjurer for your group. In fact, for all the groups."

Ren rubbed at her temples. "The Conjurers are a mess. This is the worst time to need all of us to work together."

"It's worse."

Ren's arms fell. "How can things be worse than Conjurers, Charmers, and Howlers working together against us and then scattering into the wind? I mean, at least we know *they* can work together."

Yes, they could, but only because Oswald blackmailed and scared them to death. He'd had control of Elias' mind, giving him full access to the Howlers. How terrified Garrett and his friends had to be when forced to fight us hours ago.

"Elias is dead and there are only six Howlers left alive. Our deadliest fighting force has been decimated."

Azar swore, not common for a Phoenix. Then he laughed. He laughed so hard tears ran down his cheeks. When he could control himself and wipe away the tears, he stood straight again. "You know, hours ago, this would have been the best news. We were so close to having a Darken race destroyed! Now, it's really regretful. How the tides have shifted. I never expected to see this day. Honestly, it's like we're living in some alternate universe."

I couldn't have agreed more with Azar. Sometimes I had a hard time believing I'd worked a normal human job and lived in a normal human apartment just weeks ago before being kidnapped by Falcon. Everything was changing so fast, my muddled brain had to ignore the information overload maturing had given me and try to focus on the here and now.

"Serenity, the Shadow on your team is Luna. You'll like her. She trained me while I lived with Falcon before coming here. She's one tough cookie. Made me work out until my arms and legs were jelly."

Ren rubbed her hands together. "Awesome. I like her already."

I took a page out of Arlo's book and rolled my eyes, earning me a mocking laugh from Ren. The newest memories I had of her, the ones when my children were born, remained muddled. I still had a hard time believing we were friends now, but I was so glad we were.

"Raven, your Shadow is Hawke."

"Falcon's son, right?" Raven asked.

"Yes. He's the oldest living Shadow besides Falcon. I hate to put him in a group—he has a mate and is Falcon's second in command—but he's strong and a good leader. We need him."

"Don't worry, Bri. We can handle this." Azar pulled me into a hug. "I'm just so glad we have you back."

"I'm happy to be back."

He squeezed me a bit tighter before releasing me. Raven and Serenity both took their turns giving me a hug before all leaving to their designated areas.

The silence in Dad's office scared me more than Oswald's whole army outside the compound. I'd been surrounded by my loved ones, and my new maturity had given me the confidence to do what was needed. Now, I had time to think, and thinking wasn't always good.

"Your hand is shaking." Falcon's hand reached forward. He'd slid back into the office while I worried about my choices. My mate took the paper from me. The paper listed out the names of my close friends and family who would be directly in harm's way when things went down.

"I think you're all crazy for trusting me with all this. I mean, I get your reasons, but no one should trust me. I make bad decisions, remember?"

"So you've mentioned before." Falcon leaned down and sniffed my hair. He groaned. "Charmer's lover, you smell divine. I only wish you weren't so afraid."

"We were supposed to go home, take our boys with us. Quest and Astrid were supposed to figure out their relationship. You and I should have spent years together, falling back into love all over again, having more babies."

Falcon took my hand. Darkness enshrouded us. We slid from Dad's office into our bedroom back underground. "The world hasn't ended yet, darling. Until it does, I will continue to plan for our future."

A fire blazed in the hearth. Not much, if anything had changed since I'd gone to live at the Phoenix compound. Another table had been set up by the fire. Covered plates waited for us, and the smell of food made my stomach growl. When had I last eaten? The fear and nauseousness from our situation mixed with hunger pains until one couldn't be distinguished from another.

"I'm not sure I can eat." I held my stomach. "I might throw up."

"If you don't eat, you'll faint. Then you'll be of no use to anyone. You are our leader. Your job is to remain strong." Falcon pulled out my chair. "And until the world ends, I shall endeavor to bribe myself back into the sheets with you."

"Falcon!" My cheeks blazed hotter than the fire beside me as I sat.

Falcon pulled blonde hair away from my neck. His lips tickled my skin when he leaned down and kissed me below the ear. My body buzzed as he trailed his lips down to my collarbone.

"We have one hour, my love." His voice was hoarse. "How would you like to spend it?"

CHAPTER
7

Brina

W hat I wanted came to me from a memory, well, a few memories, and wouldn't be what most women would choose to do with their devilishly good-looking mate. I shoveled food into my mouth while Falcon perused the bookshelf beside the fireplace. If we had one hour to ourselves before all hell broke loose, I was not spending the time eating.

Falcon pulled a book from one of the upper shelves. "Yes, this is the one."

"Oh? What is it?"

"A book I've looked forward to reading to you since its publication. I believe you've read it in this life, but I'm sure you'll enjoy this time much more." Falcon's sultry voice sent shivers down my spine. "Go lay down, Brina."

I obeyed. The anticipation gave me the energy to hop up on the bed and snuggle down under the covers. Falcon's bed had the buoyancy of a cloud. I sighed in appreciation.

Falcon smiled and walked to the bed. He settled in beside me with his back against the headboard.

"Ready?"

"Uh huh." My eyes drifted shut. Excitement made me squirm, and Falcon chuckled.

"Alright. Here we go." Falcon opened the book. "It is a truth universally acknowledged, that a single man in possession of a good fortune, must be in want of a wife."

Hearing Falcon read Pride and Prejudice in his deep voice sent tingles from my head to my toes. A small smile tugged at my lips as he continued. Before today, I couldn't say that Jane Austen was my favorite author, but now, she held the top spot.

The longer Falcon read, the more relaxed I grew. Sometime during his reading, I fell asleep, because when our one hour was up, Falcon had to rouse me.

"Oh gosh, I'm sorry. I didn't mean to fall asleep." Rubbing my eyes didn't dispel my exhaustion. I needed another twelve hours of sleep for that, and Phoenixes didn't need much sleep.

"Don't be." Falcon placed a kiss on my forehead. "It was a pleasure just to have you here with me. You are so peaceful in sleep, and I imagined a world where we weren't about to fight for our lives. I loved reading to you when you were pregnant with our children."

I thought back to the period of time he mentioned and smiled. "They loved to kick when you read. Of course, I thought I carried one very active baby. Little did I know what awaited me."

Falcon's sad smile broke my heart. "If I'd known the future, I would have done things differently."

I squeezed his hand. "I know."

My mate sighed. "All good things must come to an end eventually, and ours has come. We should return to the Phoenix compound to check on the groups you've put together."

"All I want to do is hide with our family until this is over."

"It will never be over as long as Chaos lives."

"Falcon, how do we stop him?" I sat up and rubbed my temples. A headache threatened to make a nuisance of itself.

"I don't know. If I did, I would have done so already. The last thing I want is Chaos anywhere near you or our boys."

"I'm sorry we didn't...you know..." My cheeks burned. I'd already slept with him before! Why was I so shy and nervous?

Falcon kissed my temple. "While I can't say reading to you was even better or just as good as 'you know,' I promise you I enjoyed myself. Don't apologize for our time spent together. If this was what you needed, then I'm glad I could be of service."

I rose and stretched. My shoulders popped. "I went up against Oswald with fury. I didn't hesitate. The Shadows and Phoenixes followed my orders."

"The Shadows love you. They will follow you to Death's door and beyond if need be. The Phoenixes respect you."

"That all makes me sound special." I turned to face him. Falcon placed the book on his nightstand where a vase of my golden feathers sat. The feathers were from a different time. One in which I believed I could do anything. "There were rules in the fight with Oswald. That's how I got away with leading. I knew the rules, and I used them. Chaos has no rules. He's guided by insanity. Who knows what goes on in that crazy mind of his. Oswald wanted to rule everyone and have power. His motive for war was very clear. I can't get a read on Chaos. He doesn't live by rules."

Falcon rubbed his lower lip with his thumb. I could imagine the wheels in his mind spinning, trying to come up with an idea.

"What if..." Falcon raised his index finger. "What if Chaos has a set of rules?"

I blinked at him. "If he had rules, wouldn't he not be Chaos who causes chaos?"

"Not necessarily. Even chaos has some sort of organization, some expected events to follow. A child makes a tall tower of blocks. The taller the tower grows, the more it sways each time a block is added until there's too much weight on one side or the other. It will fall, but the way it falls is predictable. The lower blocks have less of a chance of falling because they have a sturdier foundation. The higher bricks will fall in the direction of too much weight. There's no disputing that. But, if another tower had been built and then both fell toward each other at the same time, the blocks most certainly would hit, sending the blocks from each tower into a direction they would normally not go."

"Huh." Organized chaos. It was an interesting thought.

"Another example." Falcon lifted his leg, putting his foot on the bed and leaning forward. "Red food coloring is dropped into water. If it had a personality, it would expect to spread around the dish without hindrance. However, if a yellow drop is added, red has no choice but to turn orange when they collide."

"So, we're going off the assumption that Chaos knows the effect his type of chaos will make. Rather, he is red food coloring and he expects things to happen a certain way."

Falcon nodded. "He expects us to form an army against him. He expects us to be unable to work together. In fact, I bet he's counting on us trying to form an army only to have us tear each other apart in his planned, organized chaos."

"And we're yellow. We're another force which changes his trajectory like the second tower of blocks did. We force him to change colors without choice. That will give us an edge."

"He won't expect it. He'll need to regroup. If we could possibly put someone on the inside, someone to spy and defect to Chaos' side, we could use their information to our advantage."

The idea soured my stomach. "We can't ask someone to do that. It's probably a death sentence for anyone to join Chaos."

"No, I don't think so. Someone defecting from our side would give Chaos more leverage in his plan. The other races would be upset if someone went to Chaos. Especially if they were a big name."

"Someone like a First Four."

"Anyone in your four groups would probably work."

"I don't like it." I shook my head with vigor. I knew half the people in those groups, and too many of them were the sacrificing themself type. Half of them were my family.

Falcon slid from one side of the bed to stand beside me. He took me into his arms and ran his hand over my back. "I don't like it either, darling. We need to give them a choice, though. The little pieces of the puzzle aren't much by themself. The big picture is the most important. But all it takes is one missing piece and the puzzle is ruined. Our lack of help or information from Chaos' side is our missing piece."

"We'll bring up the plan and see if anyone volunteers." I stepped back. My eyes stung. I would not cry. There would be time for that later. But I had one more thing we needed to discuss. "Falcon, Arlo isn't well."

Falcon turned grim. "I know. He can fool everyone else, but he can't fool me."

"And yet you still allowed him to take me away twice?"

"Arlo would die before something happened to you. If he didn't think he could protect you, he would have spoken up."

I wasn't sure I agreed with that. Arlo had looked bad. *Really* bad.

"He broke up with Adler. I'm not supposed to tell anyone, but you're his best friend."

Falcon tucked my blonde hair behind an ear. "And you're worried about him."

"Both of them. Adler's mom was killed in the battle. Quest has to be upset about that, too. They're all each other has."

Falcon snorted and shook his head. "Adler is Quest's sister, no?"

"As much of a sister as Quest has right now."

"Perfect. If Adler is Quest's sister, then she is also our daughter. I'll let you share the happy news with her."

My mouth parted in shock. "We can't adopt the entire army!"

"Adler is not the entire army. She is a Charmer/Shadow hybrid who doesn't fit in with anyone else. Just as her brothers don't. Adler fits into this family as well as her brothers do, both biological and adopted."

"And you're good with Arlo dating your daughter?"

Falcon pondered that question for a moment. "Yes. He may very well not live through this battle because he refuses to sleep with another. Even kissing another would help him, but he refuses."

"You knew about that?"

"Arlo mentioned it while you were with your family in the Phoenix compound. When Chaos noticed my Shadow mark on your face, I wondered what Arlo would do. He loves her enough to keep himself from other women. He would not soon break up with her unless he felt he had no other choice. The fact he still hasn't fed after ending their relationship is testament to his ongoing love for her."

"I hope she understands one day."

"I do as well." Falcon pulled me to him. "Our time is over. We must return."

"Let's go plan how to ruin Chaos' perfect fall."

Falcon slid us back to the compound. We stood in the back of a large inside training room. Azar and Astrid stood with their team, and from the first look I had of them upon our return, I knew something wasn't right. The group of Phoenix and Darken radiated tension. I'd placed the two female Howlers on Azar and Astrid's team. The two tried not to appear afraid or intimidated as they positioned themselves near my friends. A Charmer stood near their team's Conjurer. Felicia and Cassius had done their job while I'd been asleep. Good.

"The Shadows are our weakness." The Conjurer pointed at Astrid.

"Hey—" Astrid tried to defend her kind but was cut off by her accuser.

"It's true. You can't be out in the daylight. What good are you when the sun is up? And the Howlers, they're afraid of their own shadows."

"It's not like you can see well in the dark, Conjurer," Astrid spat.

"Maybe not, but at least I can use magic to improve my vision or light up an area. I can change my surroundings. I'd like to see you do that."

Irritation made me grind my teeth together. They needed to work together. We didn't have time to fight amongst ourselves.

Fighting played us right into Chaos' hands. I stepped forward, but Falcon's hand around my upper arm stopped me.

He leaned down to whisper in my ear, so he didn't interrupt the continued disagreement. "They need to work this out on their own."

"We don't have time for quarreling."

"And Mom swooping in to help won't actually help them." Falcon's tone wasn't unkind, but the truth of them hurt. "They need to trust each other on the battlefield. You said so yourself. They need to figure this out if they're going to trust each other."

"It's not like the Charmer can fight." Astrid pointed at the woman near the Conjurer. "No offense, Laura."

"Why shouldn't she take offense?" The Conjurer was about to drive me crazy. Which one of my trusted colleagues had given me this person? Felicia or Cassius? I guessed Cassius. This girl seemed more his style, which under other circumstances I would have liked, but not right now.

"If I might." Azar broke into the heated conversation, "this energy we're expending would be of greater use if we aimed it toward defeating Chaos. Then, after he is dead or imprisoned, or whatever happens, we can continue blaming another race for not being as superior. Right now, I'd rather not die because we wasted time on a fruitless discussion about who's physically worse than the other."

The Conjurer snorted. "Why are you worried about dying? Phoenixes are reborn."

"Yeah, but if we lose, there won't be much to come back to, if it's even possible."

Azar's comment put a damper on everyone in the room. At least he'd calmed the arguing.

"Our differences are a good thing," Azar continued. "It's good that you can make light, Coral. Laura can't see in the dark. And it's good that Astrid and I can fight so we can train you in hand-to-hand combat. You might not need it, but I'm sure you'd rather have the knowledge when you need it rather than not. If you don't need training now, you will probably find yourself in a situation later where the knowledge comes in handy. Now, let's discuss our differences, but in a way which benefits us all, not destroys our peace and makes our enemy stronger."

Falcon nudged me forward. "I'll inform the other groups to come here. We might as well have this over with."

"Oh good. Then I can worry even more." Already I fought not to worry wrinkles into my dirty black shirt. I should have changed while we were at home.

I walked toward the group as Falcon slid from the room. Astrid, Azar, and the Howlers looked over at me as I approached. They had the better hearing of the group. The Conjurer and Charmer looked when the others didn't glance away from me. Coral, the Conjurer, wrinkled her nose as I reached them. Again, I wondered who had chosen this person, and how long she would last on a team.

"What's up, Bri?" Azar knocked my shoulder with his fist. "Coming to test your skills against a champion Phoenix?"

Astrid shook her head at my friend's lack of humility. "Shut your mouth, Oh Champion Phoenix." Astrid didn't wear her normal miniskirt and platform shoes. Though she did wear all black, the outfit was meant to be fought in. "Brina, what is that you're wearing?"

Confused, I checked my outfit, but it was the same one she'd instructed me to wear earlier before the battle with Oswald. "Um, clothes?"

"Yes, yesterday's clothes. Surely you've had time to change. When this is over, I might have to be in charge of your wardrobe again."

"Oh no, you're not. Not again."

"What's up, Bri?" Azar sobered the conversation. I would have rather stayed lost in the moment, pretending we didn't have a care in the world.

"Falcon and I think we've found a way to beat Chaos. We just need a volunteer."

"I'll do it," Azar spoke up fast.

I patted his bicep. "You'll want to find out what it is first. Trust me. Falcon's gone to bring the other teams here. If we're lucky, this plan could work great."

"If not?" Coral asked, looking down her tipped-up nose at me.

"Well, if it doesn't, the volunteer dies and we all mourn their loss while trying not to die ourselves. Straightforward enough answer for you?" Every member of the team shifted uncomfortably as I examined each one. "Azar is right. You *have* to work together. While I'd love to solve the feuds between the members of each team, I can't. You were all chosen because your leader thought you were the best of the best. If you refuse to work with your team, or make Chaos more powerful by causing infighting, you will be removed from your team. Don't embarrass yourself, or your people, because you couldn't play nice in our hour of need. If you can't work with the team, let me know and we'll replace you without hard feelings. You will be in the midst of the most danger. You'll want these people on your team to have your back, so don't irritate them enough that they'd rather see you gone. Like Azar said, you all have strengths to go along with your weaknesses. Determine how to use them to defeat an enemy. Do you have questions?"

They all remained silent. Even Coral had tipped her head down. My message seemed to have gotten through to her and the rest of the team. Good.

My sister Raven, Hawke, and their teammates appeared in the room. From looking at them, I could already tell they weren't having the same issues as Azar and Astrid's team. Orion, Quest, and Cassius appeared next, seconds before Serenity and Luna's team arrived with Falcon. My stomach twisted. One of these people would need to sacrifice themself for the better good of the other nations. How could I send any of them, even Coral who irritated me, into the depths of hell in Chaos' world?

Falcon joined me at my side. The teams made a semicircle

around the front of us. Sweat broke out on my forehead. I needed to speak up, but I couldn't. How could I?

I faced Falcon. "I should do it. I volunteer."

He gave away no sense of his feelings, keeping his face and voice clear of his emotions. He had to feel just as upset about this plan as me, right? "You can't. You're in charge. Besides, the plan won't work if you go. You'll just give Chaos leverage against me and the Shadows."

"What's the plan?" Cassius's arms were folded across this chest. He radiated confidence. Would he volunteer? I didn't trust him fully yet, but I wanted the chance to do so.

Falcon cleared his throat and nudged my arm. Technically this was his idea, but I had to explain the plan so the Shadows didn't seem to be running things. It was all so stupid.

"Before I explain the task needed to be done, I want to emphasize that this is strictly voluntary. No one will be pressured into doing this because there is a high chance whoever volunteers will die." A few people, mostly Charmers, cringed. There wouldn't be any volunteers from that race.

"Wouldn't it be better for a Phoenix to volunteer then?" It didn't surprise me that Coral, the irritating Conjurer, made the suggestion.

"Like I said, this is strictly voluntary. No one will be pressured or singled out to do this. Yes, Phoenixes can be reborn, but death for a Phoenix is still traumatizing. It still hurts. If the Phoenix is killed, they'll be out of commission for this fight, just like anyone else sent would be. It's not fair to limit the choice to only Phoenixes."

"Yeah, but at least they'll be reborn," Coral tried again. "The rest of us won't be."

I prickled at her audacity to continue this pointless conversation. Under Oswald, she would have kept her mouth shut. She wouldn't have objected. Now with the Conjurers free from oppressive control, it shouldn't surprise me she'd want to test some boundaries and speak up. Still, this was not the time with Chaos on the rise.

After taking a calming breath, I gave Coral a smile. "I appreciate your suggestion. Maybe after hearing what will be required of the volunteer, a Phoenix may volunteer. But, I will not single them out. No race will be treated like they are more or less expendable than another."

"You said to use our strengths." When would Coral stop? "This is a strength the Phoenixes have."

"I see your point," I assured her. "But please allow me to explain the situation before you keep throwing the Phoenixes into the metaphorical fire. Then you can help determine what would be most beneficial."

Coral nodded, and I breathed out a relaxing breath. I needed to be patient with these people, but they sometimes made it hard. A few bad apples and all that.

I spread my feet apart and clasped my hands behind my back. I needed to be strong. "We need a spy in Chaos' inner circle. The spy would give us information as we enforce the second phase of our plan."

"Which is?" Ronan, the Howler on Orion, Quest, and Cassius' team asked.

"Giving Chaos his own taste of chaos." My explanation was met by mixed expressions. Some were confused, some shocked, and even some who seemed to consider the idea. "We'll take Chaos' organized chaos and throw him a curve ball. I'm not exactly sure how yet, which is why we need a spy. Or at least someone on the inside who can exacerbate the chaos we've created on the outside."

"How are they supposed to do that?" Luna, my old trainer, asked.

"That is up to them. I cannot give them a playbook of what things they should do. All decisions will be up to them to make to the best of their ability." I paused to give everyone a chance to mull the idea over in their minds. The Phoenixes would be brave and consider volunteering. The Shadows probably would as well. There weren't enough Howlers left for one of them to volunteer and die, though after this battle was over, would we go back to destroying each other? I honestly hoped not.

The Conjurers... I couldn't guess what they would do. And, like I'd already assumed, the Charmers wouldn't volunteer. They'd be too afraid. However, I could be surprised.

"I'll volunteer."

My heart twisted, and I nearly had to lean into Falcon to stay upright when my lungs wouldn't work and Orion stepped forward. This situation had been my worst nightmare. I couldn't lose my children. This plan wasn't solid enough to send Orion in. I just got him back!

Orion stopped when he stood in front of me. He gave me a soft smile and wiped at a tear I hadn't realized had fallen. "It's alright. I'll be okay. Besides, I'm the one who makes the most sense. As a mixed child of Shadow and Phoenix who hasn't been well-received by either side, it would seem logical for me to abandon my heritage and work with Chaos."

"I could do the job as well." Quest stepped forward. Astrid gasped, and Orion shook his head.

Orion turned to his brother. "No, you need to stay here. I can do this."

"I know you can. If you change your mind, though, I could go in your stead."

Before I could cry a river and appear weak in front of the teams I'd chosen, I blew out a deep breath to settle my nerves. "Okay, everyone, return to your training. Orion, you'll decide when and how you join Chaos. Remember that you can slide, so if you need to escape Chaos, that is a possibility."

Orion nodded and the teams broke apart, sliding back to where they'd come from. Falcon took my hand and slid us to another hallway in the compound. No one else stood in the hallway with us.

Swallowing became impossible because of my grief. A

whimper escaped my mouth as Falcon tugged me to his chest. My mate's arms had always been my rock, my safety net. With him, nothing could go wrong.

I shook horribly as I sobbed into Falcon's chest. Until, when warm, wet drops hit my head, I realized that Falcon cried too. I'd been so self-centered not to realize that even though Falcon had come off as strong, he was worried about our sons and our friends, too. Sending Orion in to spy on Chaos scared him as much as it scared me. In fact, the mission probably scared Falcon more. Falcon knew Chaos, knew what he was capable of. Chaos scared Falcon, and now his son had to venture into that world. Did Orion even have the Phoenix genes of rebirth?

Time slipped by as we held each other and expressed our fears without words. The tears eventually began to slow, but we continued to hold each other, not ready for reality to set back in.

"He'll be okay." Falcon kissed the top of my head where many of his tears had fallen. "He knows we love him. I'm so sorry I allowed this to happen."

"It's not your fault. You did the best you could long ago. If you could have destroyed Chaos, you would have."

Falcon gave a soft snort. "You give me more credit than I deserve."

"Hey, the Falcon I first met only had his self-preservation and interests at heart. You would have squashed any impediment to your happiness."

"Well, you're not wrong." Falcon pulled back and winked a bloodshot eye at me. His good mood slipped. "Orion will be okay. We have to believe in him."

"Believing in someone doesn't make things work out one way or the other."

Falcon tucked hair behind my ear. "No, but it beats worrying more than you need to."

My hands slipped up Falcon's abs to his solid chest. His muscles weren't hidden by the black shirt he wore. When I'd lived with Falcon in this life, he'd dressed in a gothic style with a coat, always dressed up. Now he wore a plain black shirt with black cargo pants. He looked good. I snorted to myself. Who was I kidding? Falcon *always* looked good. Too good.

Falcon tipped my chin up. His eyes smoldered as he leaned in. His lips brushed mine.

Before the kiss could really start, Falcon pulled back. "We need to tell the others about the plan."

"You go. Tell them. I'll be right behind you. There's someone I need to see."

CHAPTER 8

Brina

Adler worked in the kitchen at the compound with other young Shadows. The other races were also represented in KP duty, though they each kept to their own kind. Shadows and Charmers didn't need to eat, but the other races did. There weren't enough young in those races to make a sufficient amount of food for the older ones who could go to battle, so the young were sent to the kitchen.

While Adler wasn't super young for a Shadow, she was too young to endure much light, which made her joining our army pointless. The Shadows she worked beside also had too much strikingly white hair to go to war. One of those Shadows I recognized as Oz, Azar's former guard. Oz enjoyed flirting with Azar, and a part of me still wondered if they would become the second interracial pairing.

Oz saw me first as I walked toward where the Shadows worked. She gave me a tight smile. Adler, with swollen red eyes, looked up as Oz waved. I finished my way to the table and took a sniff of what they were cooking.

"What is that? It smells so good." I leaned over, closed my eyes, and took another long whiff.

Oz giggled, though the sound seemed a bit strained. "It's just the prep work for potato soup. Apparently Phoenixes don't like a lot of meat, so we're working on some veggie meals for them. Do you think Azar will like it?"

Yeah, Oz had it bad for my friend. But I hadn't had a chance to talk with him about his feelings for the young Shadow.

"He'll love it," I assured her. "Adler, can I speak with you?"

"If it's about you-know-who, I think I'll pass. I don't want to think or talk about him again." Ouch. I couldn't blame her, but she had no idea how much Arlo suffered because of what he'd done. If she'd won the heart of another Darken, he might have become angry with his suffering because of her and been with a hundred women by now. But Arlo kept himself for her, even with the chance she wouldn't agree to a relationship again.

"Well, then we won't talk about you-know-who, but I'd still like to talk."

Adler put down the knife she'd been cutting potatoes with. She wiped her hands on her apron as she followed me from the room. I led the way into a smaller dining room across the hallway. Noises came from the larger dining rooms. People ate there. The small dining room I'd chosen was bright and empty.

"Hold up. I need to take care of some lights." I closed myself into the room to keep Adler safe from the overly bright room. Unscrewing the bulbs took little time. The heat from them didn't bother me whereas they would have burned another race.

With the job done, I opened the door and waved Adler inside. Adler had always been a happy person, happier than most Shadows because of her Charmer blood. Even with tears sliding down her face, Adler remained a beauty. It was easy to see how Arlo had fallen for her. Besides her good looks, Adler was also kind. In fact, I couldn't have picked a better fit for Arlo.

"I'm so sorry." I wrapped Adler in a hug. "I heard your mom was killed in the battle. I'm so, so sorry."

"It's not your fault." Adler sniffed, and her jaw quivered. "She wanted to keep me safe. And Quest. She didn't get the chance to know about Quest's family, but she would have been so happy for him."

I released her. "I never had the chance to thank her for taking Quest in. I'm so grateful for her kindness."

Adler shrugged. "It was part of Shadow tradition. We just did what we needed to do to raise children to keep our numbers up so the other Darken wouldn't attack."

What a horrible way to live. Did the Howlers now have that same fear? I'd need to talk with Garrett. As long as his people didn't kill humans and torture them, I didn't see why they'd need to be killed just because they were born Darken. Maybe that was a naive way of thinking, but times were changing—as proved by our need to fight together against Chaos. I couldn't kill the Howlers now. Not after meeting them and hearing their story.

"Falcon and I want you to know that we're here for you. You're Quest's sister, and we think of you like a daughter. Don't hesitate to ask us for anything."

"I don't want to see *him*." Adler's jaw tightened, and her eyes cooled. Arlo didn't want Chaos to think he cared for anyone. He'd done a dandy job succeeding in that regard. Adler hated him.

"You don't have to see anyone you don't want to see. I know Falcon is friends with...*him*...but that doesn't mean *he* has to come over. You're our daughter. You and your needs come first. *He* can work around those."

Adler flung herself at me, wrapping her arms around my stomach. She held me tight. While she didn't cry now, she had before, and her embrace carried across all the emotions she didn't express with words.

"I have to get back to work now." Adler pulled away, a glint of happiness in her eyes. "Be careful, Brina. Tell Quest I love him?"

"I will."

After dropping Adler off in the kitchen again and stealing a quick snack, I made my way to the conference room we'd planned our rebellion in. The team there consisted of my three sons, a Howler named Ronan, and a Charmer named Ainsley. None of them batted an eye when I entered. The furniture had been moved to the edges of the room. I took a seat in the first chair by the door as the team did what I'd wanted the others to do. They'd split in half and fought each other.

Ainsley squealed a lot. She'd been partnered with Cassius and Orion. Quest and Ronan attacked with fervor, never relenting.

"Use your voice!" Cassius yelled over his shoulder where Ainsley had ducked to escape a wolfish Ronan. Her fear was understandable. Howlers scared me to death, and being attacked by one made that fear even worse.

Ainsley cringed, closed her eyes, and stepped out from behind Cassius. A beautiful sound filled the room as Ainsley sang a haunting note. Those fighting paused.

"Kneel down," Ainsley commanded. Even I felt pressure to obey. Instead, I clung to my chair as the others in the room, including Ainsley's teammates, knelt. She blinked at them quickly, realizing her mistake. "Oh, not you guys. Sorry. Stand up."

Her team followed their orders and subdued Quest and Ronan. Ainsley beamed and bobbed on the balls of her feet as she clapped her hands lightly together.

"I did it!" she squealed. Ronan and Quest winced. "Oops. Sorry. I forgot about your sensitive hearing."

"All good." Quest groaned and stood after admitting defeat. "Just don't do it again."

"I'll try not to. I just got so excited. I may actually be of some worth in a battle."

"Only as long as you do not compromise your teammates," Cassius corrected. "Had an enemy come in swiftly who had not been under your spell, they would have slaughtered the rest of us."

"Oh, yeah. I'm sorry about that." Ainsley deflated.

Cassius then gave her a smile. "You did good."

"Good?" Ainsley snorted. "You probably could've trounced us all in a matter of seconds."

"Hey, I'm better than that." Quest stood next to Cassius, sizing him up. "I bet you that I could've taken you down before you even muttered a word."

Cassius snorted, too confident in himself to even reply to Quest's threat. Ainsley was probably right, but against Chaos, even Cassius would be hard-pressed to win.

My eyes strayed to Orion, and my stomach flipped again. And not in the good way like when I saw Falcon. He stood off to the side a bit, just as he'd done all his life, never joining the crowds and the victories. He didn't seem upset about not including himself. He'd smile as he listened to the others send verbal jabs at each other. His attention roamed the room with brows pulled together. I needed to leave. Orion was thinking about his mission to Chaos. I couldn't stand by and watch him plan for a mission which I feared would be his end. If he wanted my advice, he'd find me. Though I had little to give. I'd always been the "storm in wings blazing" type of girl. Sneaking in while gaining the trust of the enemy wasn't my strong suit.

I left the room with as much clamor as when I'd entered. Noise from Dad's office drew me next door. Serenity's team practiced there. They'd left the door open so they could use the hallway if needed since Dad's office was smaller than the conference room. This group, too, seemed to understand the aim of these teams. Serenity would attack a Howler, Conjurer, or Charmer while Luna, my former trainer, would call out corrections for those being attacked. Especially their Charmer who would, like Ainsley, squeal and run. She nearly ran me over when I peeked into the room.

"Sorry! Yah!" The female Charmer grabbed my arm and pulled so she could swing herself behind me. Serenity lashed out, and it took me a split second to realize she wasn't going to back down just because the Charmer had found cover. She intended to split that cover in half!

Ren's weapon was a fiery blade created from Phoenix power. Only the strongest Phoenixes could create their own weapons. I hadn't created one in centuries, but as Ren's sword curved down to cleave me in two, instinct kicked in. I raised both hands, bent my knees, and created the strongest circular shield I could manage in the time given me.

My arms shook as Ren's sword collided with my shield, but to my great relief, my shield held. But Ren didn't stop.

I shoved the Charmer backwards. "Get back!"

Changing tactics, my shield transformed itself into two short swords. Ren's weapon was longer, but if I played this right, I could strike at the same time I parried. I didn't count on that plan working because Ren knew all my ploys, but it was an idea until I thought of something better.

Ren slashed from the side, a bad angle for me to defend. She nearly knocked a sword from my hand.

"Careful, Bri. You would hate to lose so soon." Ren winked after taunting me.

"I may be out of practice, but even then, I'm still better than you." Which totally would have been true a few centuries ago. Now, I would be lucky to come away from this without a scratch for Falcon to worry about.

Ren tsked at me and shook her head. "Don't get overconfident, back burner."

I lunged forward at Ren's use of the very old nickname she'd given me for being second rate, the last chosen. Of course, that wasn't true, but Ren had hated me.

My arms barely held the overhead attack when I used my swords to block her. Ren's foot collided with my stomach, sending me backwards onto my back. I coughed and wheezed in a breath, but climbed to my feet anyway.

"You're not as rusty as I'd feared, but we need to work on you. Falcon won't always be near to do that bird thing you used to kill Oswald. And if you want to fight against Chaos' minions with the rest of us, you need to learn how to defend yourself." Ren attacked again, swinging her sword to chop across my body in a diagonal.

I didn't think. I didn't even know if it would work. My brain didn't have time to catch up with my body as I hopped to the side, changed my swords to a large war hammer, and smacked Ren right in the stomach. The force sent Serenity flying backwards down the hallway, and leaving me there standing while, "Oh crap," ran through my head over and over. I prayed I hadn't killed her. We needed as many strong Phoenixes as possible.

When Ren groaned after she landed and didn't turn to ash, I relaxed a little. She'd need some recovery time, but I hadn't killed her by accident.

"I hate you," Ren moaned.

"You'll get over it." With Ren alive, I smiled and walked the opposite way as Luna whistled a congrats.

Finding Raven's team took time. Time I spent fretting over Orion, Chaos, and the world. I should've stayed inside during all my past lives. Oswald still would have lost his mind, but I would've had more time with Falcon and my boys. I had no time now. A few hours. That's all I'd been given before the end of the world if we failed.

You won't fail. Joliet had joined me after I'd checked on Raven's team. Hawke and Raven were putting the others through the ringer. Their Conjurer didn't like that, but he didn't hold things up like Coral had in Azar and Astrid's team.

"I don't know about that."

You can't stop everyone from dying, Brina. Even if they don't die in the battle, those you love will eventually die. Accidents happen. Murder happens. Falcon still isn't loved by all the Darken.

I shivered. "I'm not ready to lose him."

Have you told him how you feel?

Pausing, I blew out a breath. "I don't know how I feel. My memories say I should love him, but do I actually love him, or is it a past me who loves him? It's so confusing."

Why can't you love him now if you loved him in the past? Falcon suffered while you were gone. Not like Arlo currently suffers. Yes, we can smell the Charmer weakening. Which means the Howlers soon will notice as well. But we're talking about Falcon. Has Falcon given you any reason not to love him? Why is it so impossible for your feelings to be the same as they were before and that's why you're confused?

I bit my lower lip as I began walking again while I mulled over her words. No, aside from the bad behavior at the beginning, which Falcon explained, he hadn't given me a reason not to love him. He cared for me, took our relationship at my pace, and cried with me when we both hurt. Falcon was the one I went to when fear threatened to overwhelm me. His arms were a safe place. In his arms, the world wasn't falling apart.

"Thanks, Joliet."

You're welcome. Joliet stopped. *Fargo is back. Hurry to Falcon.*

My heart leapt into my throat. Fargo had gone to check on the world. What evil had he discovered?

~

I FOUND Dad and the First Four in the outside training yard. The sun no longer shined overhead, making it safe for the Shadows to leave the building. But that same benefit for the Shadows would be a hindrance to the Charmers and Conjurers. The Charmers gave us numbers, but was it fair or ethical to send them out when the chance they'd die was high?

Fargo stood beside Falcon. The large hellhound's red eyes watched me as I jogged across the training yard. Falcon looked over at my approach.

"Fargo says the world is in turmoil. We didn't expect less. But there's a city about to fall to Chaos' minions. We need to go there and stop them before the humans are severely hurt." Falcon took my hand. "Do you think we're ready?"

The other leaders of the races watched me as I answered, making me wish I could dig myself a hole and climb in. If I asked myself why I was put in charge one more time, it would be the only thought in my head forever.

"I'm not sure about all of your people, mainly the Charmers

and Conjurers, but I think two of the teams are ready to go. I'd love to give them more time, but we don't have any."

"No," Dad confirmed. "There isn't time."

"Everyone gather as many of your people as you can. We won't take everyone, but I need your best. Arlo, I know your people still can't fight, but we need them. Even if it's just to calm the humans." Arlo nodded at my request. "Phoenixes and Conjurers should find a Shadow or Charmer to slide with. We'll take as many Shadows and Phoenixes as we can gather together. They're our best fighters. Conjurers will be a nice addition. The two groups I'm leaving have a male and female Howler just in case the worst should happen."

"Thank you," Garrett whispered. "You didn't need to worry about our species' progression, but I'm grateful."

"You're welcome. Now, Falcon will stay here along with Arlo." Falcon spun to face me, his objection written all over his face and in his red-tinged eyes. "No, Falcon. You're not going. You are the reason our people don't need to feed off humans. How they remain strong, even here where they can't go feed. They need you safe. And we need to leave some leadership here in case Chaos attacks while we're gone."

Falcon's eyes glowed brighter as he turned back to the group. He hated staying behind as much as I hated making all these decisions. No, he probably hated not helping us more than I hated my job.

"Garrett, Dad, Felicia, and I will lead our army. With any luck, this will be fast and easy. Arlo, don't roll your eyes at me." I pointed a finger at him.

He gave me a shocked expression, throwing his hand over his heart. "I would never."

I raised an eyebrow and moved on with the conversation. "I don't know what to expect, so I don't know how to command us right now. When we get there, start killing Chaos' monsters."

"That is sure to delight our 'brother,'" Arlo grumbled. "Though, I'm sure our attack will not be unexpected."

"But we *need* something unexpected." I pushed my hair away from my face. "We need a way to throw his brand of crazy off balance."

"You'll find a way." I wished I was as confident in my abilities as Falcon seemed to be.

"Good luck everyone. If you need me, I don't have a phone." Arlo tossed his across the circle we stood in. I caught it before it hit the ground. "Oh, thanks. I guess if you need me, call Arlo's phone. In the meantime, we leave in ten minutes from the front courtyard with whomever is ready. Falcon and Arlo, work with the teams that are staying behind. They have to start working together or I'll be replacing people upon my return."

The next ten minutes were a whirlwind. Falcon slid to the four teams I'd chosen to inform them of our impending battle. Arlo slid to the kitchens and nursery to have everyone hide in the safe room. Falcon and Arlo had decided that Arlo would stay with the children in case there came a need to slide them out quickly while most everyone was gone.

I stank. The smell hit me as I walked through the halls of the compound. I should have changed at Falcon's house and cleaned up. There was no use changing now. I'd only get a new outfit ruined with blood and sweat.

Falcon met me inside the doors of the compound in the courtyard. His hand wrapped around the back of my neck and pulled me to him. I didn't resist, even though we were in public. Falcon's kiss was frantic and filled with all the things words just couldn't express.

"Do not die," he growled when he pulled back, leaving me dazed.

"Uh huh." What were words again?

"Brina, there's one more thing." Falcon waited until I was lucid. "If Wraith is there, run."

"Chaos' first child, right?"

"Yes."

"How will I know she's there?"

"Trust me. you'll know." Falcon brushed my hair behind my ear. "Be safe, darling. Hellhounds howl, I wish you'd let me go with you."

"I can't."

"So you said." He glanced out at the filling courtyard. "I'd best find my charges and put them to work running laps around the training yard. They'll change their tunes about working together after that. Or they can just keep running."

I laughed. "You're evil."

Falcon's eyes lit up. "Of course I am." He leaned in and nipped my lower lip. "I'm the monster who goes bump in the night, and don't you forget that."

Dazed, in a love-smitten stupor, I couldn't respond until Falcon had made his way down the hallway toward the yard.

"Falcon!" I ran toward him as he turned. He caught me, picked me up, and wrapped my legs around his waist as I kissed him. I was about to go into battle. I'd done that many times, but this time, everything felt different. If I died, would I ever see Falcon again? Would there be a world left for me to be born into?

"I love you," I gasped when I needed to pull back for air.

Falcon's smirk turned wicked. "I know, darling." I smacked his shoulder as he laughed. The sound of his laughter made my heart warm. Falcon didn't laugh often enough. "I love you as well, Brina. Thank you for doing me the honor of becoming my mate and tying yourself to me for all eternity. Come back to me."

He set me down, spun, and walked away. My eyes pricked with tears, but I couldn't let them fall. We weren't the only couples threatened with separation. Besides, I'd make my way back to him. Death couldn't keep us apart.

In the courtyard, my eyes widened at the display Ren and her mate, my friend Dax, shared with the world. And I'd thought my and Falcon's kiss had been too much for public viewing. Wow, did they have us beat.

"Everyone ready?" I yelled as I entered the courtyard. Had it been ten minutes? It didn't matter. Time was of the essence and we needed to leave. The humans needed us.

The crowd silenced. Everyone looked at me. Conjurers, Charmers, Howlers, Phoenixes, and Shadows mixed together in the crowd. Just days ago, these groups had fought against each other. Now, they fought together.

"Look at the person on your right," I instructed. Everyone did, though some thought I was crazy due to the expressions on their faces. "Now, look at the person on your left. Good. Ladies and gentlemen, those people aren't necessarily from your species, but they are your ally. You'd better have their back, because they're hoping you have theirs out there. You're all different. There are probably hard feelings between some of you. Put that aside. Bury it. Don't think of it. Right now, we are all one race. We are the Bringers of Peace. We fight against chaos and destruction. Chaos wants to tear our world apart for his fun and pleasure. Will we allow him to destroy our world and the humans in it?" As I spoke, my voice grew louder until, at the end, they could have heard me a mile away.

As one, the group before me raised their hands in the air. "No!"

"Then grab the person next to you so we can all slide together. Guard each other. This won't be pretty."

CHAPTER 9

Brina

I'd watched riots on news channels before, but I'd never been to one in person. I never thought I would be. Quest was the Shadow who slid our entire army into the downtown of some city I hadn't caught the name of from Fargo. Quest collapsed to his knees from sliding so many people as we took in the fires, humans breaking windows, and businesses being robbed.

I came to regret my decision to leave both Falcon and Arlo behind. There were no Darken among the throngs of humans losing their minds in their rage.

"Anyone see anything?" My voice didn't carry far because of the noise the rioters were making and the sirens of the people coming to stop them.

"There!" Astrid pointed to a dark alley. I squinted to better see what she saw in the darkness. If I had trouble seeing, none of the more human Darken would see what the Shadow saw.

A dark blob moved in the alley. One of the Shadows on the fringe of the group rushed forward to grab the creature. He pulled...something...from the darkness. Whatever it was, it could change its shape. The Shadow tried to tear its head off, but the "head" would disappear only to reappear at a different spot on its body.

"I have this!" A Conjurer stepped forward, spoke a spell, and slammed the menace with light. The light dissolved the creature.

"There's another!" another Shadow called.

"And there!" came another voice.

"It's Brina! Spread out. These creatures are not actively in the fight. Don't harm the humans if you can help it. Have at least one of each race in your group. GO!"

My mom, who I honestly hadn't noticed in the throng of people, Ren's mom and dad, my sister Athena, Raven's mate Cove, and their daughter Skye rushed past me with others who weren't Phoenixes. My fear rose another notch. My family was here! Dad came with us, but I hadn't expected everyone else!

"You're with us." Cassius grabbed my arm and hauled me after Quest. Ainsley, their Charmer, hurried along with us. Where was Orion?

The Chaos monster we found changed color to camouflage itself with its surroundings. Quest's good eyesight caught it, Ainsley's voice stopped it, and my Phoenix-powered short sword killed it.

"Where's Ronan and Orion?" I yelled to the others. Quest pointed across the street before searching for the next monster to kill.

Shadows and Charmers slid warriors to different spots on this street and the next one over in our search for monsters. The monster numbers were plentiful, but fighting them didn't seem hard. The sheer number of them would be the problem in another situation, and Falcon said Chaos had *a lot* of children.

I met up with Ronan, the Howler, but Orion wasn't in sight. A sour taste entered my mouth. Was this the time? Was he about to enter Chaos' lair?

"Orion disappeared." Ronan struggled with a monster. I put Ronan out of his misery of pinning the thing down by stabbing it with my blade. "Thanks."

I stood, and the blood drained from my face. In the middle of the street, amongst the rioters and those attempting to slay the beings driving the humans into a chaotic mindset, stood a woman. Falcon said I would know Wraith when I saw her. Well,

I saw her, and she definitely gave off powerful vibes. Falcon had also said to run, but we were actually winning this battle!

Wraith held her hands in front of her. I blinked and leaned forward. Her hands curved like she held a ball. The night was too dark to see what she held, even with the fires. Until she stepped into the light. Wraith held a flowing ball of black tendrils like some sort of dark cloud.

"What is that?" Roran whispered.

"I don't—"

Wraith threw her ball. The ball barely missed our allies, but hit the building behind them, which exploded, sending glass and brick flying.

"Look out! Retreat!" I should've acted faster. Falcon had said to run, but I'd delayed.

Wraith sent another dark ball into a building down the street. The building collapsed onto a group of Darken. My heart stopped beating. Were they okay? We couldn't leave without them.

Dax, my best friend growing up with Azar, stepped forward with a golden sword in hand. Fear turned my blood to ice. What would a blast from her do to him?

"Dax! No!" I rushed forward but came to a sudden stop when a golden arrow struck Dax in the chest. He stumbled backward and collapsed to his knees. His head rose to see which Phoenix had shot him.

My eyes followed his line of sight, and I stumbled backward when I caught sight of Orion with a golden bow in his hand. He crouched in a second-floor window, another arrow notched and ready to fire. Ren screamed as Dax crumbled to ash on the ground. She rushed toward Orion, a warrior's cry on her lips, but he struck before she could get close. This time, the arrow lodged itself in her right shoulder. Ren cried out in pain, both physical and emotional.

Orion took aim again. This time, my breath caught. He aimed at me.

Ronan kicked my feet out from beneath me as Orion fired. The arrow hit a Charmer. The poor guy wouldn't be sitting for some time.

"Steady!" I yelled as our army began to run in all directions. Chaos, that's what was happening to us. "Steady!"

Wraith disappeared. My head whipped around trying to find where she'd reappear. To my horror, she appeared beside Orion. She turned my way as she held her hand out to Orion. Her face was hard to make out. Black tattoos covered most of her skin. From the distance between us, I couldn't see what the marks were, if they even meant anything.

Orion put his hand in Wraith's. She smirked, showing off beautifully white teeth. Her black robe seemed to come alive and cover them in some black mist. When the mist cleared, both Wraith and Orion were gone.

Stunned, I could only stare at the building. Orion had done his job, but...he'd *really* done his job. Dax was dead. His body was now ash on the ground. He'd be reborn, but he was a powerful Phoenix. We needed him.

"Keep killing the Chaos monsters!" Dad appeared at my side. "Do your jobs!"

I remained too stunned to be of any use. Phoenixes and Darken fought around me. They made quick work of the children of Chaos. At least I thought they did. Time slipped by as I stared into the window where my son had disappeared with Chaos' right-hand villain.

A large body appeared in front of me. Falcon took my face in his hands. His eyes scrutinized me. I watched, but my mind and body seemed numb to action.

The riot and burning buildings disappeared into darkness. Falcon's swimming pool appeared.

"Look in my eyes, darling." Falcon used persuasion to force me to obey. He gave a small smile. "It's alright."

Falcon unbuttoned my pants with one hand while he had the other around my waist. "Relax, darling. It's alright."

My pants fell to the ground, and Falcon began to rip my shirt. The part of my brain which should enjoy being undressed by my mate didn't seem to want to kick in. I didn't want to push him away, but I also didn't want to pull him close.

Every part of me shook as Falcon removed the last of my ruined shirt. He dropped the material on the floor and led me to the pool's edge. Another set of hands held me while Falcon shed his own shirt and pants. Falcon was undressing with someone else here? The idea that I wore so little didn't seem to bother me as much as the increased shaking did. I was so cold.

Falcon dove into the water. When he resurfaced, he pushed his hair back and held his arms up. "Hand her to me."

I didn't fight as whoever held me slowly lowered me into the warm water with Falcon. The shaking didn't subside. My arms wrapped around Falcon's neck, and I pulled myself closer to his body to warm up, but I still shook.

"She'll be alright?" I knew that female voice, but my brain didn't care to think about who it was. Instead, I buried my face into Falcon's neck.

"I'm so sorry, darling. Forgive me." Falcon held me to him with one arm. His other hand touched my waist. I wasn't really in the mood for sex. The touch didn't—

I cried out as an intense pain screamed in my side. My grip on Falcon slipped, but he still held me. Red blood mixed with the clear water, making my head spin. What had he done?

"You'll be alright, Bri." That voice. Who was she? She sounded nervous.

More pain in my side nearly sent me into unconsciousness. My stomach rolled, and I nearly threw up in the pool. Falcon held me to him with both hands.

"It's over. Rest. You're safe with me. Raven, call Keeve and let him know Brina is with me, and I'll bring her to the compound once she's healed.

My sister didn't respond. A door closed while Falcon treaded water.

"You'll be alright, darling."

I whimpered when I tried to reply to Falcon.

"Sleep, darling." Falcon kissed my forehead. My eyes closed without a fight. Finally, my brain shut down.

~

FALCON SAT on the bed beside me when my eyes opened. A fire didn't blaze in the hearth. Everything was blacker than night. I could smell my mate, but I couldn't see him.

The events of the attack rolled through my mind. This time, they didn't overwhelm me. Orion had done what he needed to. I'd need to speak with Ren. My son had killed her mate, and shot her. Raven had come to Falcon's pool. Why had my sister been at the pool? Falcon...

"How do you feel?" Falcon ran his fingers through my still-damp hair. At least I was warmer than I remembered before sleeping.

"I... I froze up." How could I do that to my warriors? My cheeks blazed having to admit such a thing. "Orion killed Dax and left with Wraith. You told me to run if I saw her. I waited too long. It's my fault. How many died because of my failure to act?"

I tried to push myself up. I needed to check on those the building had fallen on. My arms didn't agree with me, and I collapsed back onto the bed.

"Relax. You didn't freeze up. The attack was a success and Chaos' minions were conquered." Falcon lifted me and held me like a baby in his lap.

I'd been redressed. I wore jeans, a hoodie, and thick socks from the feel of them. My undergarments had been changed. They were no longer wet. Falcon had probably changed me. I was too tired to be embarrassed.

"My dad had to step in and give the orders. I froze up. I

might not like it, but I'm honest enough to admit to my faults. Especially when people were hurt because of me."

"You were injured. Brina. You didn't freeze up. Do you remember coming here with me?"

I squinted into the darkness as I thought back on my most recent memories. "We were in the pool. My side hurt. There was blood."

"You were hit by glass shrapnel. When I brought you here, your body was in shock. You didn't freeze up, Brina. Not the way you think you did. Your dad stepped in when he realized you were hurt, and Quest found me so I could bring you here."

"The Phoenixes have pools and heated blankets. I would've been okay there, too." Not that I didn't love the pool here, but going to the compound wouldn't have been any trouble.

"The compound is overrun with enough of the injured. Bringing you here freed up a bed for them."

"How many are injured? How many did we lose? Aside from Dax."

Falcon sniffed the top of my head. He fed on my fear. The fear that I had taken so many people into a battle we couldn't hope to win. But Falcon said we had won. How many had we lost to win?

"Astrid is keeping me updated," Falcon finally responded. "It's not as bad as it seems. Most wounds are superficial bumps and bruises. We lost three to the collapsed building. A Charmer, Conjurer, and Shadow. There are others from the collapse who are in a more critical position." He paused. I could tell by his stiff muscles that he didn't want to go on.

"Who is it? Who was hurt?"

"Felicia is not doing well. Cassius has done what he can for her. He's still trying to save her life, but the injuries are extensive."

My nose burned as I tried to push tears away. "And Cash?"

"Injured, but he'll live." Falcon kissed the top of my head. "From what I hear, you did a great job."

"I'm not sure I'd say 'great,' but the battle didn't end in disaster." My brows pinched together. "The Chaos minions weren't what I expected them to be. I thought they'd be out in the midst of the humans fighting and killing, but they weren't. They hid in alleyways and didn't always have a defined form."

"We didn't give you enough information. I'm sorry. It's been so long, I didn't even think about their forms. Chaos' children don't fight. They influence. Except for Wraith. She's a breed all her own. If we can destroy her with Chaos, we'll be set. The minions can be taken out over time. With Chaos out of the picture, no more will be created."

"How do you think Chaos will react to our refusal of his offer?"

Falcon shrugged. "I believe he was expecting such an attack. Otherwise, why was Wraith there? Small tiffs aren't her style."

"She was just getting warmed up last night before Orion showed his hand. I'm sure she would have changed the course of the battle had she stuck around."

"I know she would have. Now, I think I know a way to help you gain more of your confidence back." Falcon rose with me still in his arms and jumped off the bed, which felt weird because I couldn't see anything. "I've thought about it, and you haven't dressed your part."

"Dressed my part? Dad dresses like the other Phoenixes. I've been in black clothing ready for a fight."

"Yes, but you are not just a Phoenix warrior. You, Brina Firestorm, are Lady of the Shadows. Such a title should be worn with confidence and be appreciated by others."

"I don't need them bowing down to me."

"No, you don't. Stand here." Falcon's footsteps headed away from me. He didn't slide, for which I was grateful so I knew I wasn't alone. "You do need them to respect you. I should have thought of it before. Even amongst the Phoenixes, appearance matters. Does it not?"

"I guess so, but we all wear the same thing."

"Exactly." A flame near the hearth was lit. "It's the same reason why armies wear the same clothing and why uniforms are so popular. They create unity. You see someone wearing the same thing as you, you feel safe, you feel like you belong."

"Isn't that a good thing?"

"If camaraderie is your goal, then yes, it is. But you, Brina, were born to stand out."

The fire grew, illuminating the room. My eyes watered, so I turned from the fire with my hand raised to shield my eyes. When my eyes adjusted to the light, they zeroed in on an outfit hanging on the closet door.

Turning to Falcon, I shook my head. "I'm pretty sure this is for you."

He shrugged. "Can't it be for both of us?"

"Fine. I'll wear it. Doesn't seem like it's appropriate for battle, but..." I scrunched up my nose. "I'd like to feel pretty again."

"Change. I need to check in with your father and Arlo. You should be safe here. No one knows of this place." Rather, Chaos didn't know of our underground home.

Falcon returned to my side and placed a gentle kiss to my lips. "Do not scare me like that again. I do not enjoy smelling your blood because you're injured."

"I'll do my best. I'm sorry you were scared."

Falcon placed a kiss on my forehead. Then he turned and walked to the corner of the room by the door. He walked until I thought he'd walk right into the wall, but he slid at the last second.

"Show off." I shook my head and admired the outfit. I'd worn something similar when I first came to Falcon's.

Quickly, I pulled the hoodie over my head and shuffled out of my pants. The tight leather pants fit me like a glove. This time, I enjoyed the boots and the extra height they gave me. The black corset with the sheer skirt falling past it made me wish for Astrid's help. When would Falcon be back? I couldn't clasp this on my own.

Strong hands grabbed the back of the corset and zipped it up. My heart warmed.

"I didn't think you'd be back already. You've only been gone a few minutes."

Turning, I beamed up at Falcon. Only, Falcon wasn't the man grinning back at me.

"Hello, sister. It's nice to finally have some alone time with you."

"Chaos," I breathed.

CHAPTER 10

Brina

"I must say," Chaos stalked closer to me since I'd stepped away from him, "Falcon is a very lucky man."

My back hit my dresser. Stupid piece of furniture. My chest heaved as my breath came in short gasps. If I didn't even my breathing, I'd pass out. But Chaos terrified me. The vibe of craziness coming off him made goosebumps rise on my skin.

Chaos' constantly changing eyes took me in. I really wanted to be back in my old clothes as he stepped into my space.

"You'll want to leave, Chaos. Falcon will be back soon." I tried to keep my back straight with confidence, but my posture meant little to the insane Darken now running his fingers lightly over my bare shoulder and down my arm.

"If you think I should fear your mate, you are not as intelligent as I pegged you to be. Pity."

I swallowed hard. "What do you want?"

The pale man lifted his other hand and trailed it slowly down my other arm. "I'm not sure yet, actually. I haven't made up my mind." When his fingers reached my wrist, Chaos began to slide them back up my arm. "You lead the rebellion against me. I should kill you for it. But you're a Phoenix, so you'll only return at some later point."

Chaos laughed and snapped his fingers. "I know. You have a child. Two actually, but one is no longer your concern. The other, the one with the spider web Shadow mark, he's still fair game."

"What did you do to Orion?" I braced my arms back against

the dresser. "How did you get to him?" If Orion was safe, I needed to play along. I wouldn't put it past Chaos to lie.

"Oh, Brina." Chaos ran his fingers lightly over my skin from one collarbone to the other and back again. My heart pounded. "I am jealous of my brother."

Chaos grabbed my wrist and pulled me to him, pinning my body against his even though I pushed against him. I growled and pushed harder, but Chaos turned my body and shoved my back against the wall beside the closet. My fear rose to an extreme point when Chaos' lips covered mine.

Golden fire raced through my body. A calm came over me. Strength filled my limbs.

Chaos flew through the air when I shoved him. A golden blade appeared in my hands. Across the room, a mirror reflected my image. My eyes burned gold.

"I did underestimate you, Brina dear." Chaos disappeared and reappeared in front of me. I struck, sliding my blade into Chaos' chest. Our eyes met. He *smiled*. "Nice try, pet. You aren't made of enough light to kill me."

The blade faded, as did my hope of freeing myself from my enemy. Where was Falcon? This place was supposed to be safe!

"Now, I guess I should remove you from the premises. You're fun. I'd hate to lose you now. The others here... They're in for a surprise." Chaos laughed as a deep rumble filled the earth around us. The walls exploded inward, but Chaos and I disappeared before the debris overtook us.

My head hurt when we appeared wherever Chaos took us. Traveling with him felt nothing like sliding with the other Darken. My stomach squeezed, and I feared I'd throw up.

"Oh dear, I forget how much traveling with me harms other people. Oh dear, dear. Well, we only have to do it one more time. Before that..." Chaos slammed a syringe into my arm and pushed the plunger.

I pulled against him to no avail. "What is that?"

"Just a little something to remind Falcon of who's in charge, and it certainly isn't him." Chaos smiled like an unhinged person. Someone who didn't have it all together. The elevator didn't go all the way to the top. Not all the tools were in the shed. The light upstairs didn't work.

Chaos laughed as I staggered to the side. "Oh yes, it's working already. Now, brace yourself, this won't feel pleasant."

Traveling with Chaos didn't feel any better the second time. Especially when my head already spun before the horrid event. Chaos holding my back to his chest to keep me upright didn't help matters.

Dad, Falcon, Arlo, Garrett, and Cassius sat in chairs around the table in our regular conference room. Someone had put the furniture back after the training session had ended. Falcon rose to his feet so fast that his chair flew backwards.

"Release her, Chaos!" Falcon's eyes had flames inside them. Arlo and Dad grabbed Falcon's arms to keep him from doing anything stupid. I didn't trust myself to speak. I'd say something dumb. My thoughts were a jumbled mess. What had Chaos injected me with?

"I'm not sure you want me to do that, brother. If I let go, she's going to fall on her face. We wouldn't want that, would we? Brina has such a pretty face." His chilly fingers ran over my shoulder again, but it felt more like ants crawling on me.

"Brina, are you okay?" Falcon swore when my legs gave out and Chaos held me to him to keep me upright.

"Ah, ah, watch your language brother. Such words aren't nice things to say in front of your Phoenix family." Chaos clucked his tongue, but the noise sounded like a snare drum in my head.

"What do you want?" Falcon snarled.

"I'm so glad you asked." Chaos' bright mood would only make Falcon angrier. My mate needed to stop feeding into Chaos' ploys. But if Falcon stood here with Chaos, unable to stand or have a solid thought in his head, I'd feel just as useless and lash out. "I'm here to offer a trade. You see, I gave Brina something that should be looked into pretty soon. So, you take her place as my prisoner, and I'll let beautiful Brina go."

Both Falcons fumed. Then the single Falcon fumed. How were there three Falcons? That didn't matter. They were all angry.

"See? She needs help. It's either you or her. Which will it be?"

The ever-multiplying Falcons stood straight. Their eyes bore into Chaos as they coldly said, "Take her."

"Wait, what?" Chaos sounded as confused as I knew I should be but couldn't process words fast enough to truly understand what was happening.

"I said take her. I'm not going with you."

"You're sure?" Chaos taunted. His laugh sounded a bit hesitant, like he couldn't believe what he was hearing.

"I'm sure."

"Fine." Chaos pushed my head to the side and pulled my hair back. My throat lay exposed to him. Falcon sat down. He leaned back in his chair and folded his arms as Chaos lowered his head.

While I couldn't understand words, I could understand pain, and Chaos sinking his dull teeth into my neck made me scream. Next, I threw up thanks to the pain and the drugs Chaos had forced into my system. No one tore me from Chaos' hold as my head continued to spin and my limbs weakened with pain.

The pain didn't recede when Chaos pulled his teeth out of my neck. And Falcon still sat there as relaxed as the day we first met and he didn't love me.

He didn't love me.

Falcon claimed he did, but he didn't. He would have saved me if he did. My father was on his feet with Cassius bracing his body against the older Phoenix, but my mate sat calmly in his chair as if he had no worries in the world, and Chaos simply annoyed him like a bug buzzing around his head.

"No?" Chaos asked Falcon. "I'm honestly surprised. You still love yourself even more than you love the woman you gave

your mark to? I mean, she is beautiful. Her beauty alone would
be worth a mark just to bed her when the urge came. I haven't
had a woman in so long…"

Falcon raised an eyebrow as if he sat there bored. Blood
dripped down my throat, back, and chest, and Falcon was bored.
I closed my eyes tightly against the pain, both physical and
emotional. My head continued to spin, and my stomach threatened to vomit again. Maybe I had it wrong and when I opened
my eyes, Falcon would be fighting for me. Yeah, it was the
drugs.

I opened my eyes, but both Falcon and Arlo remained in their
seats. Cassius had pulled Dad into his, and Garrett looked on as
a spectator who was happy he wasn't in the event. Falcon's eyes
had cooled to their usual black. No emotion shone in them.

Chaos licked my neck, and I whimpered as his tongue ran
over my ravaged skin. Had he cut an artery? If so, I had only
minutes to live. But if Falcon didn't love me, was life worth
living?

"Honestly," Chaos laughed, "you don't care? After being all
fired up, I'd think me biting your mate would put you into a
rage."

Falcon shrugged. "Maybe if I were another Shadow it would
have, but I'm old enough to realize that women are a dime a
dozen. Though ones as beautiful as Brina are far more rare, I
don't mind waiting."

"Well, this was anti-climactic I do say." Chaos readjusted his
hold on me. "Well, since you do not want her, I'll throw her out
like the trash she is. Good evening, brothers. Oh, and I do hope
my new sister makes it through the night."

"She's dead." The news about Felicia's death didn't bring
emotion out of Falcon either. "Cassius took her place." Falcon
nodded to the man on the other side of Dad. "He's decently
talented, but no Oswald. No Conjurer alive can measure up to
Oswald, as much as I hate to admit such a thing."

"I see. Well, I'll be seeing you around. Toodles." Chaos

wiggled his fingers in salutation before my world twirled again as we traveled.

The wind and snow bit into my skin. I trembled so hard I feared I'd bite my tongue off. Chaos released me, but my legs had no strength to hold me up, and my mind didn't actually know where up was. I fell backward into a pile of snow.

"I would have loved to find out how pleasurable you are, dear Brina, but that wouldn't affect Falcon. If he doesn't love you, does he love your son? He would be Falcon's heir. Oh no, wait, Falcon has an older son, but he probably wouldn't give Hawke the position. Quest would be more powerful. Anyway," he drew the word out as I trembled, "Falcon has messed up my plan. But don't worry, Brina, when you're reborn and have grown into a beautiful young Phoenix again without that man's mark on you, we'll have some fun. Okay?"

A tear froze on my cheek.

"I'm so glad we were able to get to know each other better. I'll treat you better than Falcon, but I have to beat him first. Arlo is just an annoyance, and those two children pretending to lead are laughable. Your father will be easy to sway once Falcon is out of the way. Now, just relax into the snow. It'll put out your Phoenix heat. You'll go to sleep and wake up with the Griffins. It will be much less traumatic than snapping your neck." Chaos bent down and licked my neck again as I remembered Falcon killing me in such a way in a past life. I shook as Chaos' saliva froze to my skin. "I'll be looking for you, Brina."

Chaos vanished in the storm tearing through the region. The clouds were so thick, or the storm was such a blizzard, the sun barely shone. Falcon could slide in this.

The thought came of its own accord, but another tear fell as I replayed Falcon's reaction to his enemy tearing into my throat. He didn't love me. Biting a mate was an intimate moment for Shadows. Allowing another man to bite your female, especially in front of you... It was nearly inconceivable.

Despair froze me more than the storm did. In a moment of

weakness, I prayed for the storm to cover my body and hide me from the pains I'd experienced since meeting Falcon. I didn't want to die again. I didn't want to be used for anyone else's gain or pleasure. He'd fooled me, and I'd given myself to him, but I should have known he was a wolf in sheep's clothing. Falcon had kept our children as far from him as possible. He didn't love them, either. If he did, it was for his own agenda.

The fire inside me continued to cool. A thought nagged at the back of my brain that I should fight the storm and return to Falcon, but I silenced that part of my mind. Logically, I knew I'd never make my way out of this storm. Even the idea of moving made me want to vomit again.

"Brina!" Whatever drug Chaos had given me kept getting worse, because I was now hallucinating. Falcon wouldn't be in this storm calling my name. "Brina!"

My broken heart was hearing what it wanted to. Hearts were stupid. Hearts hurt you.

I no longer shivered. That was a plus. I no longer feared biting my tongue.

The snowflakes created swirls in the air when the wind died down, but then they'd be off racing again when the wind picked up. It looked like a winter wonderland laying there in the snow. If I'd been stronger, I would've considered making a snow angel. Instead, I wanted to sleep. Sleep would allow the drugs to wear off. Then, once I'd rested, I could make as many snow angels as I wanted. That sounded nice.

"Brina!" A knee pushed into my side as someone knelt beside me. "Open your eyes, darling. Shadow's wrath, open them up."

No, I didn't want to. I was tired and hurt. If anyone else had asked me, I would've tried harder, but I wouldn't try for Falcon. How had he found me? A warmth burned on my chest. Oh yes, the necklace. Always the necklace collaring me like a dog.

Strong arms lifted me. The wind didn't feel so biting now. Maybe the storm had died down. I bet the world here looked beautiful when the sun shone.

MELANIE GILBERT

~

WARM. That was the first word to pop into my head when I woke and my thought processes kicked back into gear. Pain was the next word. My head ached like someone had cleaved it in two. The bite on my neck was a dull pain, but no less intense.

I tried to move, but my weakness combined with the number of heavy blankets on me proved to be too much. Light glowed brightly on the other side of my eyelids. Too bad light wouldn't keep Falcon away.

The thought sent a stab of pain into my heart. I'd been a fool. Twice I'd fallen for his wiles. I'd died many times because I believed him. All that pain...

"Bri?" A soft hand touched my cheek. Mom! "You awake yet, Bri?"

My eyes fluttered, but I didn't have the strength to keep them open. In truth, I regretted them finding me. Rebirth would have been a new start without the necklace. I could have hidden from Falcon and Chaos, and lived a peaceful life in a cave somewhere. Or in some tiny village no one had ever heard of. I could have flown to an island no one inhabited. Even Chaos couldn't find me there, right?

"Hey, it's so good to have you back with us." Mom kissed my forehead. "You scared us. Falcon's been beside himself."

I'm sure he was. Not.

"Dad filled me in on what happened. Falcon followed your plan." What? What plan? The plan where he threw me at Chaos' feet? "You've been asleep for three days. Nearly four. Falcon has spent every minute pacing the hallway. It's too warm in this room for him. I'll let him know you're awake. He might try risking the heat for a few minutes."

No! I wanted to scream at Mom as she left my side to walk to the door. Opening my mouth took too much energy, and my head still ached so badly.

Large fingers stroked my cheek. Pain choked me. How could

he be so gentle when he'd tossed me to his enemy as if I meant nothing? He'd even admitted it. Girls like me were a dime a dozen.

Old worries Falcon had once put at ease surfaced again. He'd been with so many women before us. How could I live up to his expectations? Would he find me as beautiful as those other women? I didn't know what I was doing in bed. Would he find that irritating?

He'd calmed those fears eons ago, but now I knew they were a lie. I wasn't the most beautiful woman he'd ever met. He didn't like my innocence. I was just...average. Expendable.

A hot tear leaked out of my eye, betraying me. I didn't want to give him any more of my thoughts or life.

"I'm so sorry." Falcon's lips touched my forehead. I wanted to scream and shove him away. How dare he touch me after everything he said! But I couldn't move.

Falcon ran his fingers around the edges of the bandage on my neck. "I will kill him. I swear it."

I didn't care anymore. All I wanted was to die. Then I'd find my children and I'd hide them with me. Falcon might not love them, but I did. I'd show them they weren't alone in this world. Orion, Quest, Cassius, and Adler. I'd steal them all away and we'd be happy together. We could even take Astrid if she promised not to give away our location to Falcon. And Adler deserved better than Arlo who had sat beside Falcon as I was mutilated by a monster. He'd done nothing.

"He'll pay for what he did." And what did he, Falcon, do to stop any of it? I wanted to ask.

Hurt and anger welled inside me. The heat in my core, which had nearly died out, ignited so hot, I feared it would burn the blankets overtop me. In fact, as Falcon yowled, I did smell smoke.

"Sybil!" Falcon bellowed as the door was flung open so hard it hit the wall behind it with a loud bang.

"What's going on? What happened?"

"I don't know. Her fire has never burned me before."

Mom patted down my body, trying to put the flames out. Apparently, I had burned up the blankets. Another blanket was laid over my body. This one was lighter, but I didn't have the strength to move it. Igniting Falcon and the blankets had taken too much energy.

"She's been traumatized, Falcon."

He growled softly. "I was running my fingers around the outside of the bandage on her neck. She must have been triggered by it. I didn't mean to upset her." He cursed. "I was an idiot to remind her of what she went through. Conjurers curse me, I wish there was something I could do."

"She needs time, Falcon."

He didn't speak for a long time. "I pray she doesn't remember most of what happened, but I fear she does. I don't blame her if she hates me."

"She'll understand."

"I'm not so sure. The Brina we knew was confident. She would have led an army to destroy Chaos without a second's hesitation. This Brina doesn't think she fits into her world, like she can't measure up. She second-guesses everything: her abilities, my love for her, her place in our worlds."

"Let her rest a little longer, Falcon, before berating yourself."

"I betrayed her, Sybil. Her mind wasn't coherent, but I didn't rescue her. She will understand that." Falcon's lips gently kissed my forehead. "I am sorry, my love."

I didn't have the energy to deal with the situation any longer. Another blanket was piled on top of me. The door closed again. My mother rocked in a chair beside the bed. Falcon had a way with words. He could sweet talk anyone. I should know.

❧

THE NEXT TIME I woke up, my eyes opened easily. I pushed myself into a sitting position before I remembered I didn't want to be awake. I didn't want to face the world. And even more, I did not want to see Falcon.

"How do you feel?" Mom rose and sat on the edge of my bed while I wrapped my arms around my bent legs. My head didn't hurt as much, and the bandage had been removed from my neck. Had Chaos' bite left a scar?

In response to Mom's question, I buried my face in my knees. A whimper escaped before a sob broke free. Mom wrapped her arms around me and held me tight. I hadn't been held by my mom since my first childhood. I'd been too brave, too independent to appear weak by needing to snuggle with Mom. Now, I didn't care. I didn't care about anything.

Mom held me until I had no tears left. She only pulled back when I did. I couldn't look her in the eyes. I'd been a fool to trust a Darken. I'd embarrassed the family and doomed my eternal life mated to a monster.

"You've been out of it for five days. Falcon will want to see you." Mom brushed hair away from my face.

I didn't trust myself to speak, so I shook my head. He didn't want to see me. My fingers rose to touch the collar posed as a necklace around my neck.

"If you hadn't been wearing that, we would have lost you."

I shrugged.

"Falcon's upset about what happened."

I shrugged.

"The Shadows' home was destroyed."

"Yeah, I know." My voice sounded dead. "I was there when Chaos blew it up. Terrified doesn't begin to cover how I felt in his clutches."

"Falcon only tried to do the best thing for everyone."

I fought to hold back more tears. "Whenever Falcon tries to do the best thing for everyone, I'm always the one on the losing end."

"Bri, he loves you. Even an idiot can see that."

"Chaos is about as much of an idiot as you can come by, and

he believes Falcon thinks I'm just like any other girl he can pick up off the street." A tear betrayed me, so I wiped it away quickly before Mom could notice. I scoffed at myself. "I even felt bad for Arlo because he had to break up with Adler to keep her out of danger. He didn't help me, either."

"Falcon and Dad explained what happened."

"Then you know Falcon doesn't love me." Just saying the words cracked my heart again.

"I know Falcon was terrified with you in Chaos' hands. Abandoning you was the best way for Chaos not to kill you."

"He didn't look terrified."

Mom stroked my hair. "As the most powerful Darken, he's had millennia to practice his poker face, Brina. Just talk to him, and he'll explain."

She didn't give me a choice. Mom opened the door and left the room, leaving the door wide open, which allowed the man I wanted to see least in this world to waltz in.

CHAPTER 11

Falcon

Brina was tall for a woman. Yet, as I entered her medical room in the Phoenix compound, I'd never seen a woman so small. Her legs were bent so her knees met her chest, and her arms encircled her legs. Dark circles ringed beneath her eyes, and her skin remained pale. At least her lips were no longer blue.

She stared at the blanket on the bed in front of her with red, swollen eyes. I'd heard her sobs from the hallway. There were many names I could call myself, and deserve, and all of them were not meant for use in front of children or my precious mate.

I'd done what I thought would save her while giving us an edge against Chaos. My choices had thrown him off balance, which was what we'd been trying to do. But Brina paid the price for my decisions yet again. And we hadn't been able to use the time after her rescue to do much else against Chaos.

Fargo, I called to my bonded hellhound. *I need Victory.* Fargo didn't respond.

Brina and I existed in the same room. We'd been separated for centuries, but there had never been more distance between us than there was now.

A black hellhound appeared at my side. Joliet walked to Brina's bed and placed the tiny pup at her feet. Brina scooped the small body up and held the female pup to her chest. As if she understood the job, Victory nuzzled into Brina instead of trying to get away. In another circumstance, the sight would have warmed my heart. But now, I cursed myself again.

Thank you, Fargo. And thank Joliet. This is a sacrifice for your family, and I am grateful.

Fargo appeared beside me just as his mate had. He stepped closer so his side touched my thigh. I never met anyone as tall as me, and Fargo's back nearly reached my hip. My hellhound rarely showed affection. For Fargo, leaning against me, touching me, was the greatest comfort he could ever give.

When Brina had been holding the pup for a while, I stepped forward. Brina stiffened, but otherwise didn't react. She still held Victory and didn't shove me from the room, so I took another chance and stepped forward again.

Brina didn't look up from the blanket as I finally stopped my approach at the edge of her bed. The spot on her neck where Chaos had bitten her had healed nicely. I closed my eyes and forced my emotions to calm so I wouldn't hurt the woman I loved. All I wanted to do was throw furniture around the room and yell my anguish. I didn't deserve to do that, though. Brina had been the one harmed the most. I'd thrown her to the metaphorical wolf. She'd been torn to pieces so many times. This time had been no different except he'd left her in the snow to die.

"May I sit?" I kept my voice low. My small mate had the appearance of an animal who would run when spooked. I needed to handle her gently. Brina was tough, but this life had not been kind to her. Nor had the others before this. Her deaths still haunted her.

I had failed her too many times, but this wasn't about me. When she didn't object to my question, I lowered myself onto the bed at the end of her feet. Her lips were red now. She had scared me nearly to my own death as she laid in the snow. I had finally saved her before another death would take her from this world. But there had been a cost.

"Felicia's dead?" Brina's voice had a gravelly note to it from crying and lack of use.

Of all the news I could give her upon her waking, this was the last thing I wanted to say. But I couldn't keep the truth from her. She'd find out soon enough anyway. I would have loved to shield her from the truth, but she was my mate, not my child. She knew the unfairness and wickedness in the world. Sometimes I thought no one knew them more than she.

"Yes."

"Is Cash okay?"

I breathed out a heavy sigh. "No. While you slept, I spoke with him. As it turns out, the reason Felicia was so adamant about being replaced was because she'd accepted Cash's proposal. They'd planned to have Cash give her his mark after the battle with Oswald, but appointing her to be the Conjurer First Four put a stop to that plan. She couldn't show favoritism. Not yet. Not like I could because my people loved you."

"I wish she would have said something." Brina sniffed.

"I do as well."

Brina kissed the top of Victory's head before speaking again. "I'm sorry about your home."

I barely contained my flinch. "Our home" was how she'd once referred to it not long ago.

"Circe's spell held. While the majority of the tunnels collapsed, no one was hurt. Circe had focused her spells on the cavern holding the children. They will remain there until this war is over just for this purpose." I wanted to punch the wall. I'd protected the children by having layer upon layer of magic guarding them. But I'd left Brina alone in our room. While no one could slide there, Chaos didn't live by the same rules. "I should not have left you."

"It's impossible to go back and change the past."

"Yeah." I stared at my hands. What more was there to say? How could I help her open up? She needed to speak her mind, but Brina almost seemed dead in every way except physical. How could I bring her back to life? Sybil said Brina had been traumatized. My mother-in-law wasn't wrong, but how could I help Brina move past this and trust me again?

Being honest couldn't hurt. "Our plan was to throw Chaos for a loop, crash our tower into his."

"I remember."

"I didn't mean for you to be hurt. Our tower hit his tower much harder than expected, though his did damage to ours as well." She flinched when I brushed her leg with my fingers. "By denying you, I had hoped to keep you safe and throw him a curve ball. I know... I know it looked as if I loved myself more than you. I appeared not to care about you, but that would be the furthest thing from the truth.

"You are my heart, Brina Firestorm. I have loved you, and will continue to love you." Her chin quivered as she held the small pup. "I understand if you don't believe me. Biting a mate is sacred to the Shadows. You know this. I didn't react when he bit you. Though, I can promise you I wanted to rip him apart piece by piece. Chaos plays by his own rules. No one can predict what he'll do. It's hard to outmaneuver someone like that. Not that I wish to excuse myself. I made my decisions, and now I will have to live with them."

Brina lowered her legs, but she still wouldn't look at me. "He threatened our sons. Orion and Quest." Fear turned my blood cold. "He said something about Orion, but I can't remember what it was. I responded back in a way which wouldn't give Orion's part in this away. Chaos bought it, I think."

"Good. You did a good job."

"Don't try to flatter me, Falcon." Ouch.

"I'll inform Quest of Chaos' threat and keep him close. If there was a spot in this world where he would be safe from Chaos, I'd hide him there."

"What about with the Shadow children?" She had me there.

"If I tried that, Quest would kill me, and you know it." I gave her a small smile to ease the conversation, but she didn't look up at me.

"Isn't this room too hot for you yet?"

I had to remind myself that Brina still hurt. She hadn't had the time to process everything since she'd almost died. Her words still pained me, but again, this wasn't about me. One day, somehow, I'd prove my love to her. Even if she never came to love me again, I wouldn't change my ways. Brina had changed me, and I wouldn't turn my back on that to return to evil.

"I'll let you have your alone time." I patted the bed beside me before rising. "Please let me know if you need anything. Well, let your mom know. She can pass the word on to me."

"I won't need anything from you."

"Well, if you change your mind…"

"I won't."

I made my way to the door, disheartened more for the love of my life than for myself. She deserved a gentle life from here on out. Chaos wouldn't give that to her. If he found her now, he'd know my feelings for her. He would know I lied, and all Brina's pain would have been for nought.

"Falcon?"

I turned back at her soft call. To my shock, Brina looked up at me. Her beauty took my breath away yet again.

"Yeah?"

Brina raised Victory a little. "Thanks for this."

I gave her a small smile she saw this time. "You're welcome. And I do love you, Brina."

She shrugged. How I hated myself. I'd hurt the one person who truly mattered to me.

Brina didn't stop me again as I left the room and closed the door behind me. Truth be told, the room had taken quite a toll on my body. The heat alone drained me, but the lights glaring down from the ceiling were nearly blinding.

"How is she?" Arlo sat in the same chair he hadn't moved from since I'd brought Brina back and the Phoenixes had put her in her medical room.

I settled into the chair beside my best friend. "Not good.

Physically she's fine, if not a little weak still. But otherwise…" I grabbed my long hair and leaned forward. "Chaos kill me, I should have traded myself for her."

"And then what?" Arlo asked. "Chaos would have delighted in killing you both. He would have, too, and you know it. Brina doesn't understand what you went through to save her, but she will one day."

"I don't know about that. He broke her, Arlo. *I* broke her."

Arlo leaned back in his chair and closed his eyes. He would soon be useless to us if he wasn't already. Which was why he hadn't stood up for Brina. If he'd been at full power, I might have played my cards differently, but Arlo barely held his glamour up.

"Is she worth it?" I asked him.

Arlo cracked an eye open. "Was Brina worth a war with Oswald?"

I snorted with a small smile on my face. "Yeah."

"Adler's worth it." Arlo grunted. "Look at us. The two most feared Darken in the world, and all it took to bring us to our knees were a couple of women."

"They're worth it."

"Indeed they are. And we both might have blown our chances with them."

"It was worth it to keep them safe."

"Was it?" Arlo raised an eyebrow at me.

I leaned forward so my elbows rested on my knees. "I don't know. At the time I thought it was. Denying my love for her seemed the only way to keep Chaos from killing her."

"Yet she would be reborn."

"Her deaths still haunt her. I didn't wish to add another to the growing list. Charmers destroy me, I don't know what I'm doing. Love is much more complicated than lust. Things were easier back then."

"But not as fulfilling." Arlo closed his eyes again and rested.

"No, not as fulfilling."

Arlo and I sat in companionable silence, each lost in our own thoughts. When Brina's door opened, I stood. Out she walked with Victory in her arms and Joliet at her side. She wore Phoenix tan clothes. My mate looked better in black.

Her eyes glanced our way before darting in the other direction. Without a word, Brina set off down the hallway opposite of Arlo and me He hadn't opened his eyes. How much longer would he manage to survive? I'd need to keep both him and Brina safe.

"That went well," Arlo muttered as Brina's footsteps faded. I could still see her, but she would soon turn a corner. "Go after her. I'll be fine."

"You will rot. Can you even slide?"

"No. If Chaos should fall upon us now, I would be at his mercy."

I swore. My language needed correcting, but right then, I didn't care much. Arlo needed to be put somewhere safe. But I couldn't even find a safe place for Brina. If I could, I'd hide them both there.

"Follow her, Falc. I'm not worth your energy. I knew my fate when I chose this path." Arlo smiled sadly as his glamour fell. My friend looked worse than I thought he would.

Arlo had aged at least fifty years. His silky brown hair with its curls lay gray against his head. The hairs no longer had a shine to them. Each one looked as dead as his eyes. His skin hung off him, and his eyes were sunken.

"You've looked better." I tried to force a laugh, but it wouldn't come. Charmers were inherently beautiful. Nothing about Arlo spoke of beauty. Even his stench.

"I've felt better."

Arlo needed to be safe. The compound was not the safest place on the planet. No other places were safe, but Chaos had come here twice. Arlo was no threat to him, and Chaos knew it.

Still, he would use Arlo against me like he'd tried with Brina if he knew how easy it would be to capture the Charmer First Four. I couldn't put him with the children. Circe's magic could only hold up against so much, as much as I wanted to hide him away there. I'd risk it for my mate and children, but Arlo wouldn't agree to such a thing, so I kept my mouth closed.

"Come on," I growled and bent to pick Arlo up like a bride on her wedding day.

"Put me down. This is embarrassing. When I am stronger, I will—"

"We'll discuss it when you're stronger." I cut him off right before sliding us to the one place I could think of to keep him safe and out of Chaos' eyesight. The small cabin did not have good memories. Thankfully it still stood after Chaos brought down the tunnels beneath the ground around it.

"Oh, I recognize this place. Lovely home you have here, Falc."

"Shut up, Arlo."

I laid my friend on an old pile of blankets I'd once used to keep Brina a little warm when she was my captive. Back when I didn't know what love was, only the carnal desires of my heart. The blankets probably had holes from moths and bugs, and the amount of dust and dirt would clog most people's lungs, but I needed to leave quickly before Chaos found me. How did he always know where we were? How had he found my underground...

Orion.

Cursing below my breath, I did the best I could to cover Arlo so his weakened body would stay warm. He couldn't come down with a human illness, but I didn't need to leave him in discomfort.

"Go, Falc. Brina needs you. Keep Adler safe, please."

"I will do my best, old friend."

Arlo snorted as I smiled. "I look that bad, huh?"

"Were you entombed with the Pharaohs, or is this a new look you're going for?"

He smiled but his eyes remained closed. "You are a good friend, Falc. I'm sorry I doubted you."

"I would have done the same if our roles had been reversed. Though, I would not have thrust balance down your throat. Still, you weren't wrong."

"Get out of here."

"Rest well."

Arlo didn't reply. He let out a deep breath and relaxed into the blankets. Adler did not understand the sacrifices Arlo made to be with her. Things with Chaos needed to end, and soon, because Arlo wouldn't be the only Charmer weakening.

I slid from the cabin to the conference room we'd been using. Cassius, Quest, Astrid, and Adler were the only occupants of the room. The men paced the length of the room while the women sat at the table, not any less worried than the men.

"How is she?" Cassius saw me first. "How is Mom?"

Mom. I loved that name for Brina. She had such a large heart to accept all of her children, biological and not, without question of who they were or what they'd done. My mate saw the good in everyone. While she worried about trusting Cassius—she hadn't told me, but I knew her well enough to read her expressions—she gave him as much trust as she could. He'd fought well with his family, Quest had assured me, and his concern for Brina was honest and genuine. If there was a role Brina loved more than being a warrior, it was being a mom. She'd joked about adopting the entire army, but I had a feeling if Brina could, she would. Her heart was filled with love, and she wanted to spread that to all so they wouldn't feel alone like her sons and daughter had throughout their lives.

"Physically she's well," I answered, stepping further into the middle of the room instead of the dark corner I'd appeared in. "Maybe a bit weak, but not harmed. Mentally...emotionally..."

"You did what you needed to," Cassius assured me. He was

the only one of my children present when Chaos had brought Brina to this room.

"I am beginning to think I should have tried something else."

Cassius gripped the back of a chair and leaned against it. "You cannot reason with crazy, evil men, Falcon." He grinned. "Dad." My heart warmed at his correction. How I loved Brina Firestorm for bringing light and warmth to my life. For giving me a life worth living. "Trust me. I lived with Oswald for years. To win against them, you have to use manipulation yourself. Besides, you threw him the curveball we needed. Well, the start of what we need. We need to find another way to throw his tower out of its current trajectory."

"How do we do that?" Astrid crossed her arms over her chest. "Orion's our best bet, and no one has heard from him. Have you?"

I shook my head. "No. How did he learn the location of the Shadow home?"

Quest ducked his head. "I might have taken him there once so he knew what his new home was like. I'm sorry."

"Don't be."

"If I hadn't, Chaos would not have found Mom." Quest grabbed his hair and continued to pace. "It's not your fault. It's mine."

The door opened and we all turned to see Keeve walk in followed by Garrett the Howler. Keeve stopped just inside the doorway.

"I'm sorry. We're interrupting. But I have things we need to discuss." Keeve waved Garrett to stop when he tried to back out of the room. The Howler, he was about on par for Brina's adoption qualifications: alone and needing someone to have his back. But he had one major flaw which wouldn't win him over: he was a Howler, and Brina feared them.

"No, you're not interrupting. We were just discussing Brina's condition, but the conversation is finished. We need to focus now that she is awake and moving around." I shoved my hands into my back pockets, a rare move since I normally did not wear modern clothing. I preferred a more gothic approach to my wardrobe. "We are at a strong disadvantage, and our time to stop Chaos is coming to a close."

Quest stopped pacing to stare at me. "Why?"

While I didn't look directly at Adler, I kept her in my peripheral vision to catch her reaction to my words. "Arlo is useless to us now. His people will be weakening soon if they haven't begun to already. They need to feed, but if they're following the safety protocols, they're not leaving the compound. Obviously Phoenixes are not an option for them. The other Darken could be, but I will not command anyone to sleep with a Charmer. If anyone wants to kiss them, that would help a bit, but neither of these are long-term fixes. Soon we'll be down both Howlers and Charmers."

"But how do we kill Chaos?" Astrid asked. Beside her, Adler had stiffened when I mentioned her ex-boyfriend. If only my lovely daughter knew how much that man loved her. I feared she would not live long enough to know.

"I don't know." My shoulders fell. I'd wracked my brain for hours to remember enough about our time with Chaos previously to find a weakness of some kind. But Chaos was wily and ever-changing. Throwing him off balance seemed the only option for now.

"Could you and Brina do that bird thing again?" Adler suggested.

"Not likely." For that to work, she needed to trust me. Our energies needed to mix. The act was as intimate as making love to her, and Brina was not ready for either. Not after Chaos had nearly killed her, and I'd denied my love for her. My heart sang, because I'd rescued her in time. Whereas before, I'd always been minutes too late. However, my brain knew the person I'd saved was not one I deserved because I'd harmed her. I'd promised to do whatever I could for her to believe I wasn't a monster. But the truth remained the same: I was a monster through and through. Nothing could be done about that fact.

"If we could pin him down somehow, we could kill him like his children," Cassius suggested. "The Phoenixes and Conjurers succeeded in killing them pretty easily."

"It won't work." A small voice behind me rocked my entire world. Brina stepped further into the room when her father and Garrett moved over. Victory remained in her arms, and Joliet stood at her side. "I stabbed Chaos with a sword made of my power. He laughed and said it wasn't 'light enough,' or something like that. I think I'm remembering that correctly. Maybe the phrase is wrong, but it was something about light. The wrong kind of light?"

Our children—Astrid included, because I had no doubts she and Quest would make a pairing—walked to Brina and embraced her one at a time. Even Cassius held her tightly to him. How I longed to do the same, but she wouldn't allow such a thing, and I had no way to prove my love to her. Not yet, anyway. But I would because I would never quit trying. I'd die before she suffered again. I should have when Chaos brought her here.

"Any ideas about what that means, Falcon?" Brina glanced my way at her father's question. I hadn't taken my eyes off her. I had no plans to.

"None, but it's something to look into." My continual stare made Brina fidget and grasp Victory tighter, but I wasn't about to change my focus. She and her happiness were my number one priority. Brina was right. I could not change the past, but hell-hounds howl, I'd make for darn certain she never hurt again.

"You came here for a reason, Keeve?" Even as I addressed her father, my eyes didn't stray. Brina was the most beautiful woman ever born. She was not average. Her type of beauty was not a dime a dozen. How I wished she'd believe me.

"I agree with Falcon. We need to make our stand, and soon. Two of my compounds were destroyed, killing all but a handful of Phoenixes who just arrived." Keeve's news created a pit in my stomach. We were down Howlers, many Phoenixes, and about to lose our Charmers. I couldn't see how this would end well. All I wanted to do was hole up in my room with Brina and make love to her until the end of the world came. Because of my actions, I would never be that close to her again.

Maggots eat me alive, I needed to find a way to end this.

CHAPTER 12

Brina

Falcon hadn't stopped staring at me since I'd entered the room. If I had the ability to slide, I would have exited the room by now. Joliet could take me away, but my children were here, too. And I'd started us down this path with a plan which hadn't done much good for us. I deserved to hear all the bad. I'd done this to our people.

"I'm sorry my plan wasn't good. I—" Falcon appeared in front of me. I had no time to move as he speedily wrapped his strong arms around me and held my body close to his. Poor Victory squeezed out from my hold before she was crushed.

"I do not care how much you don't want me near." His possessive growl created a shiver up my spine. "You are my mate, a mate I love above all others. I messed up, but I will not let you suffer because of it. You are not at fault. You are brilliant. We are not dead yet. Keep your head up, Lady of the Shadows. You changed not only one man, but many. Your goodness will help us win this. I am not worthy of you."

I shouldn't have, but I leaned into his embrace. I'd always found safety there, and this time was no different. His tight hold seemed to heal bits of the brokenness inside of me. But I shouldn't lead him on. I shouldn't allow him to hurt me again.

But I was tired. Tired of pain, tired of evil, and tired of death. Felicia was dead because of me. I'd seconded Falcon's decision to make her the First Four of the Conjurers when she should've been mated to Cash.

Falcon released me when I pushed my hand against his abdomen. He slid back to the other side of the room. My stupid heart felt bereaved by the distance, but my brain knew better than to allow him to manipulate me again. I needed to stay strong. No more—

A bang echoed around us. The ground shook, sending us all to our knees. Joliet grabbed Victory and the two disappeared. Falcon slid to cover my body with his as another boom, this one louder, vibrated my body.

"It's Chaos!" Falcon yelled. "Get your people out of here! Keeve, Quest, Adler, Garrett, Cassius, command your people to flee. Those who can slide should take those who can't."

Quest slid away with those Falcon had singled out, leaving Astrid in the room with us. Falcon called her over. He tucked Astrid underneath him so she lay beside me.

"I need to get the two of you out of here." Falcon did as he said, sliding us to a place I recognized and didn't want to be.

A body lay on a pile of blankets. He looked old and dead, but maybe it was my lack of sight in the dark. If that was his stench, though, he smelled dead.

"It's Arlo." Falcon pointed to the body. "I'll be back with Quest, Adler, and Cassius as quickly as I can and anyone I can save."

He slid away before I could protest. What would I say? Stay here with me because you don't love me and I'm stupid for caring about you? He would be returning with my children. I needed my children safe. My gut already hurt worrying about Orion. Why hadn't he reached out to us yet? Tell us how to stop Chaos? I couldn't worry about my other children in harm's way. Adler wouldn't be reborn. Quest had Phoenix DNA, but was mostly like Falcon, so I didn't know if he would be reborn or not. Cassius only had a tiny bit of my DNA. His chances at rebirth were nearly the same as Adler's, in my opinion.

And then there was Garrett, who'd also been sent from the room. A man with no family and few Howlers to lead. My heart hurt for him. Had he lost family during Chaos' attack? Was he close to the other Howlers who'd survived? Would the Howlers even survive this? We should have brought Garrett with us.

"Bri," a hoarse voice called. I barely heard him over the pounding of my heart.

"Arlo." I crawled over to him. Because of the lack of light, I couldn't make him out well, just his shape and the gray of his hair. "Are you alright?"

He gave a wet laugh and choked. "Not really. I'm sorry I couldn't help Falcon save you. If I'd been stronger, he might have tried to free you."

"Might have. Probably not. He doesn't think much of me."

Arlo started into a coughing fit. Astrid helped me raise him up to a sitting position. Where Arlo had once been strong and charming, he was now skin and bones with quite the stench. Astrid tried to breathe through her shirt to hide the smell.

"I'm sorry," he wheezed.

"It's okay. What can we do?"

"Nothing." Arlo squeezed my hand. "No, there is something. Tell Adler… Tell Adler I loved her with all my heart."

Arlo passed out after that. We laid him back down as he wheezed with every breath. How could he continue to survive this? He wouldn't die from lack of feeding. How was that possible?

"But he broke up with Adler. Quest told me." Astrid's confusion was logical. Anyone who knew would be confused. "Quest is irate, but he hasn't said anything to Falcon because of Falcon's relationship with Arlo. And, I think Quest might still fear Falcon a little."

My heart was sad for Quest. He shouldn't fear his father. But he'd lived in fear of the man for hundreds of years.

"Arlo loves Adler. He won't sleep with anyone or betray her in any way to strengthen himself. He broke up with Adler, because he was afraid for Adler's safety should Chaos find out about her. He didn't want Chaos to use her against him. Kinda like what Chaos did to me."

"That had to terrify Falcon." Astrid's comment surprised me.

"I mean, he did seem upset at first, but the—"

"Yeah, I know. Cassius told us. I still believe Falcon had to be terrified for you."

I shook my head. "No. He said he didn't love me, that I was just above average, but he could find another pretty easily."

"Oh shut up, Brina." I balked at Astrid, though I couldn't see her well in the darkness. "Arlo broke up with Adler because he was afraid for her. He loves her, but he hurt her to save her, and now he's in this state because he won't betray the love he has for her. If Falcon didn't love you, he wouldn't have searched for you for hundreds of years. He would pressure you to sleep with him, and not go at your pace. He'd be sharing his bed with a bunch of whores. Not waiting patiently for you to decide to finally let him have you.

"Did the way he reacted with Chaos hurt? Yes. Did it save your life? Yes. Did it tear Falcon apart? Oh, I can guarantee it most certainly did. That man is head over heels in love with you, Brina Firestorm. Should he have tried something else instead of what he did? Maybe, but he was only given seconds to decide on a plan that wouldn't end in you dying yet again and living with horrible memories of another death."

Astrid's words had grown louder and quicker the more she spoke, and when she finished, she took some deep breaths to calm herself.

"The fact of the matter is, Brina," she went on when she'd calmed down a little, "Falcon only had you for a limited amount of time. He's trying to do the right thing, but he doesn't always know what that is. Plus, he's a guy, and sometimes they don't think things all the way through. But Falcon is trying. And finally having you back only for two of his enemies to kidnap you has to torture his mind. Give him some grace, Bri. He's trying."

I mulled over her words as a tapping finally caught my attention. After a few short seconds, I realized it was Astrid's foot. I was such a jerk. While I was worried about my family, Astrid was also worried about hers. Including Quest.

"He gave me his mark," Astrid whispered into the silence, except for her foot tapping the dirt.

Shock stole my words. What? Was she saying Quest had given her his Shadow mark?

"He's wearing mine, too." Yes, that was exactly it!

Joy rushed through me. "I'm so happy for you, Astrid. Both of you."

"And he mates like a Phoenix. Just so you know." Astrid had never sounded so smug. My heart warmed for my son and his mate. They were perfect for each other, and Astrid had never made him feel bad about being different. Except that he wouldn't sleep with her, which made more sense after I remembered I'd had babies.

"I really am so happy for you."

"Do I have to call you Mom?" Astrid's nose had turned up. I could hear it in her voice.

"If you called me Mom, I'd probably fall over from shock." We laughed. "But, if you wanted to," I said seriously, "I would be honored."

"Thanks, Bri."

"You're welcome. And don't worry. I'm sure they'll all be okay." They had better all be okay.

But as the minutes stretched on, even I began to fidget. Where was Falcon? He was supposed to be bringing our children here. Surely the attack from Chaos had to be over by now. So where were they?

The worst came to mind. I could picture my family spread around the courtyard, bleeding and torn apart. Chaos laughed as he stood over their bodies.

"I can't sit here any longer." Astrid rose to her feet. "I'm sliding in to check on them."

"Don't leave without me."

"Are you kidding? If I take you, Falcon will kill me."

"Astrid, I'm not asking." I grabbed any part of her I could reach in the darkness. "I'm going. Falcon can keep his temper to himself."

"Fine. Get ready. Here we go."

CHAPTER 13

Brina

I knew things would be bad before we left. What we found was worse than I'd imagined.

"Well, this is why I couldn't slide into the compound." Astrid had slid us into a crop of trees near the compound. The sun had set, but the trees gave us cover from enemies. "I don't see any signs of Chaos. Anyone, actually."

"I don't, either, though my eyesight isn't quite as good as yours." Squinting into the darkness didn't help me see any movement. All my worst fears screamed that if Falcon hadn't come back to us, he wouldn't be. The thought made me sick. If Astrid was right, I'd kept my loving mate from me for our last moments together.

Sliding across the field to the edge of the compound didn't improve our perspective of the pile of rubble my once-home now was. From the close-up view, though, I could make out people in the darkness. Bodies, rather. They laid on the ground unmoving. Some were covered in large boulders. The scent of ash floated on the breeze.

"Quest!" Astrid rushed off to climb the nearest pile of rubble. Her eyes would see more than mine, but I saw just fine as I climbed over what had once been a wall and into the courtyard. I knew it was the courtyard because of its position, not for its lack of debris. How would we find anyone under all this rubble?

Astrid continued to yell for Quest. If I opened my mouth to call for my family, I'd throw up. A metallic scent turned my stomach. Blood. There was so much of it, even I, a Phoenix, could smell it.

Astrid screamed, a sound which froze my heart and curdled my stomach. I rushed over a pile of rubble to her side. How I wished I hadn't when I arrived to find her clinging to Quest's body. His eyes were open, but unseeing. A large gash covered his forehead. There was more blood, but I didn't dare look as my world crumbled, and I collapsed beside Astrid.

Quest hadn't turned to ash. He wouldn't be reborn. My baby I just got back wouldn't call me Mom ever again.

The thought tore a sob from me and destroyed my hope. Somewhere in this pile of rock, I was sure to find Falcon, Cassius, and Adler. My Phoenix family would be reborn if Chaos didn't destroy the entire world first.

I couldn't see through the tears which streamed down my cheeks. My hand gripped Quest's pants as Astrid screamed her pain into the darkness. Her pain finally pulled me out of my downward spiral of grief. She'd been his person for centuries, and they had finally solidified their relationship before being pulled apart forever.

Astrid didn't fight me as I pulled her off Quest and into my arms. My daughter-in-law held me tight as we both cried for what we'd lost.

"Astrid, take him back to the cabin." I nearly choked as I spoke. My voice didn't sound right to my ears. "I need to find the others."

She pulled back and wiped at her eyes. "I can't leave you alone here. Quest would kill me for that. Besides, taking him away won't bring him back." She whimpered again.

"Go, Astrid. If Falcon slides there, he'll need to know where I am. He'll panic if we're not there, and I'm not sure Arlo is awake to tell him. If he even notices we're gone." And I did not need her seeing anyone else's lifeless body. Already, I doubted I could handle seeing such a thing, but I needed to protect Astrid. She was the last of the family I had. Maybe we were the last of our kinds along with Arlo.

We'd failed. *I* had failed.

"Okay." Astrid sniffled and wiped her eyes. "But I'll be back for you soon."

"I'll be here."

Astrid squeezed me one more time and then knelt beside Quest's body. She closed his eyes. If not for the blood, he could pass for being asleep. Though Shadows didn't need sleep. With that thought, Astrid and Quest disappeared.

Alone with only the full moon as company, I became aware of just how quiet the field around the compound was. The moon allowed me to see heads and limbs sticking out of the rubble all around, and even more bodies scattered into the field. Most were Charmers and Conjurers who couldn't slide away from the danger. I wouldn't find the Phoenix bodies, but their ashes blew around in the slight breeze, drawing my attention to the piles which used to be my friends and family.

Overcome with grief, I could only sit on the pile of rubble and look around. I'd sent Astrid away so she wouldn't see more dead people she knew, but as I sat there, I couldn't bring myself to search the debris. For now, my loved ones had a chance of being alive. If I found them here, that hope would vanish.

More tears came as I mourned my son. Our memories together played in my head, making the pain worse. I bit my lips together to keep from screaming as Astrid had.

"Oh dear. What have we here?" My blood ran cold at that voice.

Chaos stood ten feet from me. I raced toward him, growling my pain and calling forth a sword. Stabbing him hadn't worked, but surely I could take the neck off the snake.

Pain lanced through my right shoulder. The blade fizzled out as I caught sight of Wraith and Orion. Orion held a golden bow. My knees gave out. Orion wasn't supposed to join Chaos. He... he was supposed to help us.

"Falcon is full of surprises, isn't he?" Chaos knelt in front of me. Terror choked me. If he touched me, he could take me anywhere. He could take me back to the snow. I'd die.

But…what did I have to live for now? Besides Astrid. My jaw tightened in determination. Astrid was enough to fight for my life. I wouldn't leave her alone.

I stood. "You haven't won yet, Chaos." Appearing strong and intimidating didn't really work with an arrow sticking out of my shoulder, but I did my best.

Chaos rose to his feet and smiled. "Dear Brina, your home is in ruin along with the other Phoenix compounds I've gotten my hands on. The others will fall soon enough." His smile fell to a scowl. "I'm tired of the games. This is my world."

I smirked, which in hindsight wasn't smart. "I thought you liked games, Chaos. Or do you like them only when you're winning? Are you afraid of something?"

Chaos smirked and disappeared, leaving Wraith and my son. Neither smiled. Neither said a word. When Orion moved, his bow evaporated and he placed his hand over his heart. Then Wraith took his arm, and they were gone.

With a groan, I reached up and tried to feel if the arrow went all the way through or was lodged deep instead. My hand came away bloody, but the arrow had gone through my shoulder. If I broke the shaft, I could pull the arrow from my shoulder and begin to heal.

A growling in the silence made me still. Oh no. Not another Howler come to kill me. The blood had to be calling them. I… I couldn't die that way again. And I couldn't leave Astrid alone.

"Brina!" Rocks exploded as Falcon, wings and all, burst out of the rubble which had been piled on top of him. My knees went weak in relief. Falcon slid and caught me before I fell to the ground. Blood covered his face, and his clothes were ripped and bloody as well.

The sight of the blood reminded me of Quest, and I buried

my face into Falcon's neck. He held me, keeping clear of the arrow still stuck in my shoulder, as I cried.

"Mom?"

I spun to find Cassius climbing from the same hole Falcon had come from. While he appeared beat up, he didn't have any life threatening wounds.

My wings erupted from my back, and I sailed over to Cassius. He winced as he put weight on a leg, immediately taking the weight off it.

"You're alright?" I searched him for less obvious injuries but couldn't find anything serious.

"I'm okay. Dad saved me." Cassius' eyes swung to Falcon who flew up behind me. "Thank you."

"I will do anything it takes to protect my family." Falcon's head turned, taking in the destruction. "Adler didn't stay long. Her people fled fast without taking many with them. Cowards. Quest—"

"Is dead," I squeaked out before my throat closed up again.

Falcon stilled his search of the area. Pain filled his face. My mate squeezed his eyes shut and took in a deep breath.

"Astrid took him back to be with Arlo." My voice shook as I found a way to speak again. "They exchanged marks, and they have a Phoenix mating, but…he didn't turn to ash."

"We need to remove this." Falcon kept a clear expression as he reached for my wound. "I'm sorry for the pain."

"It hurts less than losing Quest."

"I understand." Falcon grabbed the shaft and paused. "This is a Phoenix arrow."

"Orion shot me."

Falcon cursed and broke the arrow. I tried not to cringe too obviously, but didn't succeed. Falcon pulled the two pieces from me, and Cassius placed his hands on either side of my shoulder. He whispered a few words, and the pain receded until there was none.

"I'll give the two of you some time." Cassius slipped away, examining the debris for others who could still be alive.

"Falcon," I whimpered and threw myself into his arms. He held me tightly as we both cried together again. "It's my fault. It's all my fault. I'm so sorry!"

Falcon shushed me quietly as he rubbed my back. "It's not your fault. Quest should have slid to safety."

"But he was here and not with Astrid. I should have stayed with you and made them leave. They shouldn't have been separated, but I was only thinking about myself and my pain. I was hurt and let that make my decisions."

"Oh, Brina." Falcon's voice cracked. He kissed the top of my head and held me tighter. "If anyone is to blame for that, it is me. I love you with my whole soul, as worthless as it is. Your blood... I never wish to smell it again, or taste your fear, unless I am the one biting you."

"Falcon, bite me?" My lower lip quivered as I pulled away from my mate. I was too miserable to be embarrassed about my request. I'd lost one son, was confused about another, and struggled to believe my mate loved me. "I don't deserve it for doubting you."

He shushed me again and lifted me off my feet. Falcon sat on a large boulder and held me in his lap. I used my arms, which were wrapped around his neck, to pull myself closer to him.

Falcon began to hum. When the humming grew louder, he began to sing. My eyes stung at the Phoenix lullaby coming from my strong mate. As he sang, Falcon rubbed circles into my back. The two of us remained quiet as the stars slid across the sky after he'd finished.

"You sang that song to our boys every night when they were in your womb. Your mother sang it to you when you were a young Phoenix." Falcon broke the silence as the sky began to lighten gradually in the east. "You looked forward to the day you could sing the song to our baby when he laid in your arms."

Tears streaked my cheeks again. My head hurt nearly as bad as my heart from all the tears.

Falcon gulped. "We will save Orion. I promise you. We will not lose him as well. And we will keep Cassius and Adler safe. I will not let you lose another child." Falcon's deep voice had risen an octave as he spoke through his tears.

My mate's large hands pulled me back and tipped my head to the side. He growled deep in his chest as his nose ran along my neck, sniffing my blood. A pleasurable shiver ran up my spine, and my heart clenched in guilt. Quest was dead. How could I allow myself to feel anything but pain right now?

"You have been bitten by too many other men since I found you. It will *not* happen again." Falcon bit into my neck where it met my shoulder as my heart swelled with the amount of love and possession in his voice.

Joy spread through me. The heady feeling didn't dampen the grief in my heart, but my connection to Falcon grew. He held me to him with such care, with such gentleness, tears pricked my eyes again. We'd lost Quest, and the hole he left in our family would always be there, would always hurt from how much we missed him. And even though I had no idea how we would beat Chaos, Falcon and I together could make it through anything.

Falcon licked my neck when he finished. He hadn't drank long, but the blood would help him heal.

"What do we do now?" I asked as Falcon held me to him. Phoenixes didn't need a lot of sleep, but everything we'd been through had sapped my strength. Right then, I needed Falcon to be the strength I lacked. "How many escaped this disaster?"

"More than you think." Falcon's reply eased some of my fears. Even a small army was better than four people facing off against Chaos. Well, five if we counted Orion, and right then, I wasn't sure if we should be counting him with us or against us.

My brows drew together in thought. "Before he left with Wraith, Orion put his hand over his heart. I wouldn't have noticed except it was very intentional and not in line with his actions. Do you think it has a meaning? I mean, Orion hasn't helped us at all. What is he waiting for?"

"What if he can't help?" Falcon suggested. "What if he's under too much scrutiny? If he left, such an action could get him killed when he returned. Don't lose faith in him, Brina. I think he was trying to tell you he loved you. Why else cover his heart? And his arrow didn't pierce your other shoulder."

I rolled out of Falcon's arms and began to pace. My thoughts all came back to Chaos and that line about light. What had he meant about light?

"I think Chaos can die," I surmised out loud. "And I think he even knows how. Otherwise, why mention that I had the wrong light to kill him, or not enough light?" Turning to my mate, I drew in a deep breath. "I think we need to find whatever light it is that Chaos is talking about. Grab Cassius. We need to get Adler to Arlo. The two of you need to remember everything you can about Chaos and light."

"I've been trying to remember since you mentioned it. I can't think of anything."

"Well, think harder."

CHAPTER 14

Brina

Falcon slid away and returned to Cassius and I with Adler at his side minutes later. Cassius hadn't been successful at finding another living soul. He had only survived because Falcon had shielded them both with his wings, but the rocks had left Falcon unconscious until he smelled my blood.

Adler took Quest's death as badly as the rest of us had. Falcon had to catch her as well, and held her as she cried for a long while. No one rushed her. Grief couldn't be rushed. Cassius held my hand while I tried to hold back my own tears. There would be time to grieve when Chaos was dead, and Wraith along with him. So far, the being Falcon feared hadn't done much except steal Orion away. What was she waiting for?

"We need your help, Adler." I cringed at what I needed to request of her.

"Mine?" She blinked at us. Cassius shrugged. He didn't know what the job was.

"Adler, you are the only one who can do this. I can't emphasize that enough." If she refused, I wasn't exactly sure what we'd do.

"I'll do what I can," Adler offered.

"Wait until you hear what it is," Falcon admonished, wrapping his arm around her shoulders to keep her upright.

Adler's wide eyes watched me, anticipating what I would

say. She wouldn't like this, but maybe once she understood, she'd come around.

"Adler, we need Arlo back on his feet." She scowled when I mentioned his name. "Listen, Arlo loves you. He loves you so much, he hasn't fed since he met you. Even after he broke up with you to keep you out of Chaos' sights, he hasn't fed. He refuses to be with anyone else because his heart belongs to you. Adler, Arlo's not doing well." My voice hitched, and I cleared my throat. "You won't recognize him. He's so tired he can't open his eyes. He can't slide. He's helpless. All because he loves you and wants you safe."

While I talked, Adler shook her head. "Why didn't he tell me? Why make the choice for me? I could've helped him and stayed away."

"Because Falcon and Arlo want to do what's best for us, but they don't always know how. They're learning. And they need our patience while they do. Sometimes it takes a lot of patience." I winked at Falcon with a half smile. As much as I wanted to trust Falcon outright, that he loved me, part of me still worried I was falling for another ruse.

Adler bit her lower lip as she contemplated my words. She glanced toward the east and winced. "Take me to Arlo. We need to get out of here before the sun comes up. I'll do my best to help, and then he and I are having a loooong chat."

"Thank you, Adler. I wouldn't ask this of you if it weren't necessary." I took her hand while Cassius held my other hand.

Falcon slid the four of us to the dark room where Arlo lay, and where Astrid cried while she held Quest's head in her lap. Cassius created a ball of light when we'd arrived so he could see. I nearly asked him to put the light out. Arlo looked near death, making Adler gasp. And Quest was dead. Seeing him again struck my heart. He wouldn't be coming back.

I blew out a breath to keep from crying, reminding myself again that I could fall apart later. Adler and Arlo needed me now, and I needed a plan. I'd lost one, maybe two sons. I wouldn't lose the other two children I'd been blessed to call mine.

Adler sank down next to Arlo and ran her fingers through his dismal hair. She spoke to him quietly while rubbing his arm. Tears again fell from her eyes. One day, we would all be happy. Chaos would be gone and we'd have our lives back. Most of us. Astrid would mourn her love for eons, as I would mourn the loss of my baby.

I turned to Cassius to stop the waterworks from flowing again. Crying wouldn't save us. I needed to keep reminding myself of that, or I'd fall apart and lose this battle to save the rest of my family.

"Hey, Cass. Do you mind if I call you Cass?"

He smiled. "No. I don't mind. No one has given me a nickname before. Even if it's shortening my name. I like it."

"Come here." I held my arms open, and Cass didn't hesitate to wrap his arms around me. "How are you? How's your leg?"

He pulled back and stepped on the leg again. The wince wasn't as defined as when he and Falcon had first come out from under the rubble, but he still hurt. "I'm afraid I won't be of much use if we need to move quickly. My magic is useful, but I am not."

"What kind of light spells can you do?" Maybe it was Conjurer light we needed, not Phoenix light because we hadn't been created yet when Chaos was born.

"Many. What kind of light?"

"I don't know. Chaos just said something about light."

Cassius leaned against the wall. "Maybe that bird thing you and Falcon do that I've heard talk of. You were lit up."

I shook my head. "I think that would work on his children, but my gut tells me it won't work on Chaos."

"And your gut tells you that my light will work on him?"

"It's an option." I shrugged. "Right now, we're almost out of those. I mean, Phoenixes were created to bring light to the darkness of the world. Chaos is darkness. Why won't my weapons kill him? He didn't fear me at all."

Cassius' brow furrowed, and he began to chew on a thumbnail. I whacked his hand out of his mouth. He raised an eyebrow at me.

"It's a bad habit. Germs and all."

Cass smiled at me. "You know I can't get sick right? But thank you for your concern."

I shrugged. "Well, one day you might meet some female, and you want your nails to look nice, not rough and bitten. Trust me."

"I'm not sure I'll live long enough to meet a female, but I will take your words into consideration."

"Thank you."

"Charmers don't have light," Cass changed the subject back to the problem at hand. "Neither do Shadows. Shadows are the absence of light. A black light? Maybe that's it? Howlers lack light as well."

"Maybe it's the color?" I suggested. "Howlers don't like all colors of light. Maybe it's something like that."

"What is this about light?" Arlo's voice sounded exhausted. When we looked over, he sat propped up against a wall. Adler held his hand.

"Chaos said light could kill him, or rather not my light. What light does he mean?"

Arlo closed his eyes. Adler leaned forward and kissed his lips. I diverted my gaze as Arlo deepened the kiss. Awkward. But the kiss did its job.

"I'm not sure," Arlo answered when he had the strength. He rubbed at one of his temples. "I feel like there's something at the edge of my mind, but I can't recall what it is."

"Keep trying, please."

Falcon wrapped his arms around me from behind. His lips kissed my neck. Cass smirked and created another light in his hand. He changed it from one color to another.

"Maybe this will work." He snuffed the light out. "I'm going to rest. Unlike the rest of you, I need sleep."

Adler continued to help Arlo improve. I owed her. *He* owed her as well. A favor and an explanation from his lips. This keeping their women at a distance that Falcon and Arlo decided on was all for naught. Though, since Chaos had kidnapped me, we were lucky he'd never found out about Adler.

I braced myself to look in the dark corner of the small room. Astrid no longer cried as she ran her fingers through Quest's gray hair. His spiderweb Shadow mark stood out even more than normal on his deathly pale skin. One of his shirt sleeves had been ripped off. On his shoulder a lightning Shadow mark had been etched into his skin. Astrid's mark.

My heart ached for them. As a Phoenix, I'd taken death and rebirth for granted most of my life. Forever separations weren't a part of my young years. Not until I met Falcon. His mortality hadn't quite sunk in during our time together. Now, the reality that Falcon could leave me forever scared me to death, too. Quest had left me forever. He'd left Astrid.

I raised my head and breathed fast and hard. I would not throw up. Not now.

"Where are the others who didn't die in the attack?" I asked to distract myself. Falcon had said people got away, but how many?

"The Charmers and Shadows scattered to Arlo's house and mine. Each took Conjurers they could grab ahold of, and Howlers if they were present. Phoenixes retreated to another compound for the moment."

"Chaos is headed there," I interrupted Falcon. Fear raised goosebumps on my arms.

"I know. They weren't planning on staying long. Some slid with the Darken. To be honest, it was a run-for-your-life situation, and the goal was to just get out."

I forced my shoulders to relax. "I know. I'm not trying to judge."

"It's daylight out." Falcon slid down the wall, and pulled me down to sit on his lap. "We're stuck here for a while."

"Maybe not."

Falcon arched an eyebrow at me. "How so, darling?"

"It's time to end this, Falcon. Take me to the place where Chaos tried to kill me. If it's dark there, you should be able to slide."

Falcon growled. "You are not going there again."

"Falcon, please. Take Cassius with us. At least he can help defend me."

"I will gladly protect my mother," Cass volunteered. "I have nothing else to live for, as pathetic as that sounds."

"I want to go, too." Astrid's eyes glowed red like Falcon's did at times. Anger surged through her. "I want to end the man who stole my mate and my happiness."

"I think I should not go." Arlo tried to rise and fell back against the wall. "While you're gone, I'll keep thinking about the light thing. I swear I know something. The memory is just millennia old."

"We'll check back when we're finished talking with Chaos."

"You're what?" Arlo barked.

Falcon stood and set me down as Arlo continued to sputter until Adler told him to stop. Cassius took my hand and Astrid took Falcon's other hand. I braced myself for the cold, and was rewarded with a snowstorm. The sight of snow did not bring back good memories, but we weren't here to walk down memory lane.

"Chaos!" I yelled into the wind.

"Is he really going to hear that?" Astrid griped, sounding like her true self for a moment. But it was only a moment because her heart ached too much to be whole again.

"Chaos!" I yelled again.

"There's no reason to shout, dear."

I reached for Astrid and held her back as Chaos came into view in the storm. My stomach twisted as Wraith and Orion followed him. Orion appeared too at ease with his place beside the devil lady. The way he bumped into her, on purpose, put a sour taste in my stomach. When he leaned over and whispered in her ear with a smile, my steps faltered. She slipped her hand beneath his shirt to rest over his abdomen.

We'd lost Orion. Unless we could kill Wraith, she would keep him under her spell. He hadn't been trying to communicate with me. I'd envisioned what I wanted to make me happy. How many times did I have to act the fool?

"You called, Brina?" Chaos smirked when he noticed where my attention lay.

"It's time to end this, Chaos."

"I do so very much agree, my dear. You're joining my side then?" Chaos' smile remained unhinged.

"You killed my son." Was it my imagination, or had Orion flinched? "I will not be joining you."

"Suit yourself."

"We'll meet you after the sun is down in the field outside the Phoenix compound you destroyed. Bring as many of your children as you'd like, and we'll end this." My voice was as cold as the weather around us. This time, the Phoenix heat inside me burned hot. I wouldn't be freezing to death today.

"I'll pencil you into my schedule. Isn't that what the hip people say?" Chaos laughed and disappeared with a wave of his fingers as if saying "toodles!" once again.

Orion bent and kissed Wraith. *Really* kissed her. Falcon wrapped his arm around my waist and held me tightly to his side. When Orion finished his kiss, he walked across the snow to us.

"Orion." Falcon nodded to our son.

"Quest is dead?" The question held no concern for his twin brother, just asking if a rumor was true or not.

"Yes," Falcon answered. I didn't have the stomach to say the word.

Orion nodded, turned, and walked back to Wraith who held her hand out to him. He took it, and they were gone.

The four of us took hands again, and Falcon returned us to the little cabin. Cassius shook the snow off himself with a large shiver. The snow didn't seem to bother the Shadows, and the heat inside me melted it from my clothes and skin.

"Don't doubt him, Brina," Falcon advised. "What you see is not always the truth. I recently taught you that lesson, for which I am still sorry."

"We need to send word to the others." I set about making plans instead of dwelling on Orion. I'd lost Quest. Orion seemed to be gone, too. If we couldn't pull off a miracle, we'd all be dead soon enough. Then I would be reborn and live forever without those I loved. My mate and children would be gone. The fear took my breath away as Falcon helped Arlo stand.

My hands trembled, but I tightened them into fists so no one would notice as Falcon began to give orders. "Go to your people, Arlo. Explain what is happening. Take Cassius with you in case you run into trouble. Brina and I will gather the Shadows and those with them. Tell them to be prepared to fight for their lives against Chaos and his followers."

Arlo swore. "Falc, we can't beat them."

"Well, I'm not going down without a fight." Arlo flinched at Falcon's raised voice. Falcon let out a steadying breath. "I'm sorry. My family is in danger. I cannot protect them."

"You're forgiven, old friend." Arlo and Falcon laughed. There had to be an inside joke there. At least they could find a tiny bit of joy in a moment of pain and fear. "Be careful, Falc."

"You, too. Protect my daughter." Falcon hugged Adler who held him tightly.

Arlo blinked at him. "Your daughter?"

"My daughter," Falcon confirmed. "Do not hurt her again, Arlo, or I will break every bone in your body."

Arlo nodded slowly. Of anyone in the world, he knew his friend's threat to be real. Falcon would protect his children with his life if needed. He'd done so with Cassius, protecting him from rubble which should have crushed him. He would protect Adler and her heart from anyone, even his best friend.

Adler took Arlo's outstretched hand. I didn't want her to go. I wanted my family to stay together. That family also included Arlo. He was as much a brother to Falcon as anyone could be, but not enough for Arlo dating Adler to be weird.

The two disappeared. Astrid had Quest's head in her lap again. Her tears had returned. My heart ached, oh how it ached. Quest was brave, and kind, and protective. He was everything I'd want him to be if I raised him myself.

I knelt in front of Astrid. The blood had dried on Quest's face and in his hair. If I didn't hurry, I'd fall apart again and be useless in our current war.

"Stay with him, Astrid." I covered her hand with mine. "Stay with him."

"But you need everyone, and it's not like I can help Quest." Her voice cracked. "I should have gone with him."

"Your head won't be in the battle. You'll get yourself killed. Quest would kill me if I allowed that to happen."

"He's dead, Brina. What else is there to live for? I might as well die in battle." Astrid, the Shadow who never cried or showed much emotion besides sarcasm, let out a small whimper.

"I know he's gone, A-s-don't-shorten-my-name-and-add-another-s." Astrid snorted as I reminded her of the conversation she and Quest had had the night I met him. "In all seriousness, though, I cannot lose you, Astrid. And maybe that's selfish, but you are my family. I love you, and I cannot lose you because of grief. I need you to stay with him."

Astrid nodded with tears in her eyes. "Okay. I'll stay."

"Thank you." I stood and returned to Falcon's side. He reached a hand out, and I took it. "Together forever."

He nodded. "Until death do us part."

CHAPTER 15

Brina

We stood in the field outside the pile of rock which used to be my home before I met Falcon. Our army consisted of any Phoenix or Darken we could find. While many had died at the compound, I had a feeling many of the Darken had fled for their lives.

My parents had survived the battle at the compound. Raven, Cove, Noa, and his mate Gemma had not, among many other Phoenixes. Hawke and his mate Sadie survived, though many of their friends, and her family, had perished. People in the field cried. We tried to rally them, but after the destruction they'd seen, they had little hope left.

"Did I bring them here to die?" I whispered to Falcon.

"You brought them here to save their families."

"But I don't even have a real plan."

"You taught the Phoenix couples how to fly as birds. The Conjurers will produce as much light as they can. If we lose this battle, it is not because we did not try. And it is not because of anything you did or did not do. This is not your fault." Falcon squeezed my hand.

Off to the side, Garrett the Howler First Four stood by himself. He was what remained of his people. We'd been too late to save the others. Falcon had encouraged him to remain behind with Astrid to keep his kind alive, but Garrett had refused. He would fight this battle with the rest of us and not hide as a coward, or so he'd told Falcon.

My heart hurt for him being all alone. As the last of his kind, he had no one to watch his back. At least no one like him. If we won, once he left the battlefield, there would be no one ready to hug him and rejoice that he'd made it through alive. He'd go home to no one. His days would be spent alone. While the other Phoenixes and Darken had lost loved ones, they still had people to cling onto when this ended. Garrett would be as alone as Cass had been for years.

"Garrett," I called the Howler over.

"Brina, Falcon." Garrett nodded his head to each of us. "What can I do for you?"

Falcon shrugged and stared down at me. I hadn't talked with him about this, so I hoped he'd agree. He'd volunteered to take Adler in, and he'd agreed to take Cassius as our son. We had some sort of connection to each, but Garrett was all alone. He had no one.

"Garrett, if we survive this, we'd like to offer you a place in our family." I held my breath to see how each would react. To my relief, Falcon turned to Garrett for an answer. A tiny smile raised his lips. No, I did not plan to adopt the entire army. I just wanted to be a mom and care for those who had no one else, or who were a bit different and needed love.

The Howler stood there with confusion written all over his face from his wide eyes to his open mouth. "You're serious? I mean, I get why you adopted Cassius. It was kind of a no-brainer. But I'm not any part of you."

"No, but no one deserves to be alone. Besides, Adler isn't ours biologically. And we have a child from each race except yours. Might as well have a full deck, right?" Garrett laughed at my joke. "But really, Garrett. We mean it. You need someone to have your back. A family to have your back. We want to be that family."

He scuffed his boots against the ground. "My kind haven't been nice to you, Brina. I've heard rumors and stories. Why would you want to adopt a Howler when they've killed you so many times?"

"You didn't kill me, Garrett. I can't judge a whole race based on a few. Yes, when you changed your form before, it freaked me out a little, but it's not your fault. The more you shift forms, the more I'll grow used to it. I *want* to grow used to it." I stared at the western horizon as it continued to darken. "Life isn't as black and white as I thought it was. Phoenixes aren't strictly good while Darken are strictly bad. There are good and bad mixed into the bunch. Yes, my kind were created to fight against evil, but that doesn't mean we have to destroy entire races of Darken while the humans slaughter and hurt each other. If a Darken hurts a human, I will end him or her, but I will not kill them just because they exist. Never again."

"You're a good soul, Brina." Garrett gave a small smile. "I would love to consider you family."

"You'd better survive this then." I choked up.

"I'll survive." Garrett turned and shifted as the hairs rose on the back of my neck. Black blobs slid across the ground toward us. In their midst walked Chaos, Wraith, and Orion.

"Now is when we find out where he stands," I commented to Falcon.

"Do not doubt him."

"He killed Dax."

"Believe in him, Brina."

Chaos minions erupted out of the ground. A chill swept all warmth away. The grass beneath our feet frosted. My breath escaped in a cloud as a howl ripped through the air from a gust of wind which threatened to tear my feet out from beneath me. Hopelessness threatened to break my heart, but Chaos couldn't be allowed to win because of the fear he placed in our hearts.

"Attack!" I held a golden sword above my head for all to see because no way did they all hear me above the wind.

I stabbed a dark blob. Another took its place. This one appeared humanoid and punched me in the face. Falcon tore its head off in retaliation before jamming his own blue flaming sword into the monster.

"Well, that's a nifty trick." His sword matched mine as far as I could tell with a quick examination after he pulled me to my feet. The monster's punch created tears in my eyes, which I rushed to brush away.

There wasn't time for Falcon to respond as more blobs appeared. The ground seemed to hold an endless supply of monsters. When one disappeared, another took its place. Sweat dripped down my back as I worked my way through monster after monster with Falcon at my side. I lost track of Garrett. He wouldn't be able to kill these things by himself. I prayed he'd found someone to help him.

There were screams and shouts around us. The minions outnumbered us greatly. Chaos wouldn't need to touch us. His monsters would overwhelm our small army before we had a chance to fight Chaos face to face.

A burst of golden light to our right blinded me for a moment as a Phoenix pair soared through the darkness, killing any minions they touched. Another pair began to destroy the enemy together on our left. For the first time in a while, hope returned to my heart. If we could take out enough blobs, we could beat Chaos. At least we'd have a chance to try. This plan could actually work!

The first Phoenix couple were slammed out of the sky by a dark ball of energy. I gasped. That hadn't come from a minion. Azar's parents Maxine and Byron landed beside me. Each rolled a few feet before stopping, eyes wide but unseeing. The sight left me nauseous, reminding me so much of how we'd found Quest. My best friend's parents disappeared into piles of ash the way I'd hoped my son would but hadn't.

Blood drained from my face as my head swung to take Wraith in. Another black ball floated between her hands. She'd knocked Maxine and Byron from the sky with one of those things, the same way she'd brought down the buildings on top of us. My hope faded. If we didn't take out Wraith, we'd never destroy Chaos. He used her as a shield, or rather a weapon to keep us at bay while he watched. His gleeful smile took in the destruction around him. Chaos didn't care about his so-called children. He delighted in the discord they created, but they meant nothing to him.

Wraith's second ball flew through the air as I took down another Chaos monster. The other Phoenix couple barely missed being struck. Together, they'd veered out of its path. My distraction found me on the ground with a monster's foot on my chest. However, I could still see the black orb as it missed the Phoenixes and soared straight toward a group of Darken fighting Chaos monsters. A ball of light collided with the darkness before it had a chance to strike. My eyes flashed to where the light orb had originated. Cassius held another ball, ready to take on Wraith. She smiled in anticipation.

A howl—animalistic and not weather-related this time—reached me before the monster on my chest was torn off. Garrett dragged the beast away with his teeth. Azar struck the monster with a sword, and my heart warmed that my friend still lived.

"Up you go." Azar pulled me to my feet and jumped back into the fray.

I turned my attention back to Wraith. She'd flung another black ball at another pair of Phoenixes. I squinted in her direction. Where was Orion? He wasn't at her side. My eyes darted to Chaos. Orion wasn't anywhere around him, either, but Orion was dressed in black and had black hair. He'd blend into the night. While my eyesight was good, I didn't have the sight of a Shadow. Orion could be in the crowd fighting.

Another monster appeared before me. He sprung up from the ground and kept going and going until he stood at least ten feet tall.

"Well, at least you don't have teeth." The creature didn't seem bothered by my comment as I struck. He moved faster than I anticipated, dodging to the side. I changed tactics, switching my weapon to a crossbow. The arrow loaded, I took aim and shot.

"What?" I cried as the monster created a hole in itself for the arrow to fly through. Thankfully the arrow wasn't a waste and hit another of Chaos' monsters and not one of the Darken who were our allies. I would have died if it hit someone on our side. I'd need to be more careful.

The monster moved fast, faster than my Phoenix genes helped me move. One moment I stood there gaping at the hole, the next, I flew through the air, having been kicked by the monster. Impact with the ground hurt. Rolling for yards hurt more. Everything ached when I came to a stop on my stomach. My head spun, but otherwise I had no life-threatening injuries.

In the distance, Falcon yelled. The large monster evaporated into the air, having been taken out by my mate. I groaned and tried to rise. Everything hurt too much. That monster had kicked the entire front of my body with its foot...leg...whatever it had used. While nothing was broken, the breath had been knocked from me along with incurring pain.

A Darken slid in beside me. I smiled at the black hair until I recognized Orion. My smile faltered at his scowl. His hand wrapped around my arm and pulled me to my feet. The grip he had on me tightened, forcing a hiss from me. Dizziness caused my strength to lack when I tried to pull my arm from him.

Orion slid us to a copse of trees beyond the battlefield. He slammed my back into a tree and lowered his face into mine.

"I don't have long. You need to listen to me, and I need you to trust me."

"You killed Dax." I winced at the pain my body was in. The Phoenix fire within me wanted to defend against the threat Orion posed, but I wouldn't hurt my son without cause. Even if he'd yet to give me a reason that proved he didn't work for Chaos. "You shot me."

Orion gave a growl and leaned around the tree to view the battle. "We don't have time for this. He'll notice I'm gone. I killed Dax or purpose. He agreed before we even went to that fight that he'd be my way into Chaos' clutches. Serenity knew as well, but there's no time for you to verify that.

"And I'm sorry I shot you. And I'm sorry I pushed you into the tree. I'm scared and out of time. You gave me this job. Told me to do whatever I needed to do to find you a way to win. Well, I found it, and I need you to trust me." Orion's frantic explanation ended with his eyes wildly searching the area past the trees again.

Trying another tactic, Orion closed his eyes and breathed deeply in and then out. His eyes reflected tears in the moonlight. "Is Quest really dead? Is it my fault? Did I kill my brother?"

My chin quivered. "I'm sorry, Orion. He's gone. I don't know what happened. He was crushed when the compound collapsed."

Orion's face screwed up. "Mom, please trust me. What I'm going to ask of you won't be easy. I understand if you doubt my allegiance, but I'm on your side. I always have been. Please, trust me."

Memories of Orion being teased when I first arrived at the Phoenix compound assaulted my mind. No one had trusted him enough to give him a mission because he was different. He'd leaned on me as a friend. When he found out I was his mother, I'd offered him love without judgment. I'd offered that same love to Adler, Cassius, and Garrett. Yet I'd doubted Orion so quickly. Orion was my family. We wouldn't win this unless we acted together, as a family.

I smiled and reached for his face, cupping his cheek with my hand. "What do you need me to do?"

Orion grimaced. "You really aren't going to like it."

"It doesn't matter. I trust you, Orion. What do you need me to do?"

ORION HADN'T BEEN KIDDING when he said I wouldn't like his plan. After hearing the details, I fought not to question my trust in him. His pleading eyes and vulnerable heart were why I agreed to the worst plan imaginable, and without many details.

All Orion had instructed me to do was allow Wraith to take me near Chaos with a blade to my neck. That was the entire plan. No other explanations beyond, "Let your enemy put a knife to your throat and pray." I was to trust Orion after the explanation because we didn't have time for questions. He told me the plan at top speed, and I had five scary seconds to decide.

"You trust her?"

Orion nodded. "I do. Please, trust me." He glanced around the tree again. "We have no time left. If you want Chaos dead, trust me."

"But Chaos said something about light—"

"Brina!" Orion's eyes pleaded with me.

"Okay. I'll do it." Against all better judgment, I would trust my son and allow my enemy to hold a knife to my throat beside a crazy man.

"Thank you." Orion's shoulders slumped forward in relief. "I need to go fight. Please, Mom, don't worry."

He slid away before I could comment that his request that I not worry was impossible. I'd lost a son already. I would worry about my family and friends for the rest of my life. Which, I feared, wouldn't be long because Wraith appeared in front of me as scary as ever. This close, her deathly white skin made the black marks on her face even more defined. There was no pattern to the marks like a Shadow mark. Blackness crept up her neck and into her jaw like veins, or branches on a tree. More marks came from her other ear across her cheeks. She had no eyelashes. Her eyes were black.

"Come on." Wraith pulled me away from the tree and spun me around. Her blade, cold as ice, rested against my neck as the trees disappeared. We reappeared beside Chaos. Wraith pushed

me forward a step with her while my head spun from the unnat-
ural sliding, or whatever they did.

Wraith's fingers slipped into my hair so she could hold my
neck back. Something inky curled around my wrists, pulling
them together. It had to be the blackness she made her balls
from. The blade cut into my skin, sending warm blood down my
neck. I shivered, completely at Wraith's mercy, and prayed Orion
knew what he was doing and hadn't been tricked by our enemy.
That seemed just Chaos' brand of evil.

"Enough!" Chaos' voice boomed over the field. "This is your
last chance. Give your allegiance to me, or Brina dies along with
the rest of you."

A growl from the field let me know how Falcon felt about my
captivity. He needed to keep his wits about him, so he didn't
ruin Orion's plan. What the plan was from here on out, I didn't
know. This is where things got sticky. I was supposed to trust
Orion and the monster holding a weapon to my jugular without
knowing a plan. How was this supposed to help us?

Doubt wanted to enter my mind, but I shut it out. I *had* given
Orion this job. While we hadn't gotten help from him yet, this
was the moment we needed it.

"No one?" Chaos laughed when our army stood among his
so-called children, not giving into his wishes. "Well, I thought—"

Wraith moved so fast, even Chaos didn't have time to react.
He didn't have time to defend himself as Wraith pushed me
down and stabbed Chaos through the heart with her blade.

"You dare!"

Orion appeared at Wraith's side. He smiled at her. "You can
do this, Miriam."

"No!" Chaos bellowed. He tried to kick Wraith, but Orion
stabbed him with a Phoenix sword. Orion's sword wouldn't kill
Chaos but it stopped him from attacking Wraith.

"Do it, Miriam!" Orion bellowed as he held Chaos.

The black shackles which had held me dissipated as a light

grew around Wraith's hand. Chaos fought against Orion as the light brightened.

"No!" Chaos faded in and out, like he was trying to disappear but couldn't. His cries soon became screams as the light around Wraith's hands began to move into Chaos. I squinted to see what was happening. Wraith shifted enough for me to see that she pushed light into the blade she'd held to my throat. The light spread out from the wound to soon engulf Chaos to the point I couldn't look at him anymore.

With a final scream, Chaos' cries ended. The light faded as speckles of it fell to the ground where Chaos had once been. Wraith's shoulders rose up and down like she breathed hard. She and Orion stared at each other until Wraith began to laugh. Laugh! The sound was filled with pure joy as my son gathered her into his arms.

"You did it, Miriam. I knew you could." Orion pulled back and smiled at Wraith...Miriam?

Wraith pushed away and disappeared. Orion's eyes widened. He hadn't been expecting her disappearance.

With their boss and his second-in-command gone, the Chaos monsters fled. The warriors of our army kicked back into action to kill as many as they could before the monsters disappeared. I didn't have the strength or capacity to help them. My body still hurt from being kicked like a football by the last monster I'd faced off with. Not to mention the exhaustion taking over me caused by the stress of trusting Wraith not to kill me.

When the last had been killed or fled, the field again silenced. Shock had stolen words from my mouth. Chaos was dead? How? The light? What had Wraith done that I hadn't been able to do with my sword?

Strong arms encircled my waist and pulled me back against a broad chest. "Orion, explain." Falcon's tone was not harsh, but Orion flinched anyway.

"Wraith is not what she seems," Orion answered softly. "She is not what you were made to believe her to be."

"What is she then?" Arlo had appeared at my side.

Orion stared at the place where Wraith had once been, but was now gone from. "She was created to stop the Darken. To stop Chaos. But he discovered her before she was ready. He used his power to blacken her soul. With Chaos out of the way via the First Four, another group of people were created to keep the other Darken in check. The Phoenixes."

"Wait, something was created before us?" I shook my head as Orion's words tumbled around in my head again.

"Don't keep us waiting," Arlo complained. "What is she?"

Orion swallowed hard and turned to us. "She's an angel."

"A what now?" Arlo sounded as shocked as I felt.

Orion grew frustrated, running both hands through his dark hair. "An angel, Arlo. A-n-g-e-l."

"No need to be smart, kid."

"That was the light Chaos mentioned." A different light went off in my brain. "She was created to destroy him, so my power couldn't."

"Yeah," Orion answered. "I'm sorry killing Chaos took so long, but after learning from Miriam what she is, convincing her she wasn't too far gone to do what she'd been created to do took time." He smiled at me. "Thank you, Mom, for trusting me. I know it wasn't easy and you still had your doubts. But thank you."

My throat thickened as tears stung my eyes. "I'm sorry I ever doubted you."

His smile was sad. "Honestly, that was my point. If you doubted me, then Chaos would trust me more. But you believed in me when I needed you to."

"I won't doubt you again. I promise." My heart ached with regret, but I couldn't change the past. The future would find me to be a better mother.

"It's alright." Orion walked to me. Falcon retreated as Orion wrapped his arms around me. "I'm not upset with you. You've been so kind to me since we met. I'm grateful. I don't hold a grudge. All I hope is that life is kind to you from now on."

Orion released me and winced as he took a step back. "I'm sorry about the Shadow's home. I really hope I didn't kill anyone by giving the information to Chaos."

"No. All is well," Falcon answered.

Orion nodded. "I know the Phoenixes at their compounds are dead, but they'll be reborn. I wasn't so worried about them." He gave a soft laugh. The sound warmed my heart.

Astrid appeared at my side. I gaped at her.

"You're not supposed to be here! We left you with Quest. For all you knew, the battle wasn't over yet!"

"Brina, relax."

"I will not! You are not supposed to be here!"

"Quest is gone."

"Yes, I know my son is dead."

She shook her head with a growl. Typical Astrid. "No, Brina, he's gone. He's ash."

CHAPTER 16

Brina

"He's what now?" When we'd left, Quest's body had been whole and not ash.

Astrid smiled as tears slipped down her cheeks. "He turned to ash, Brina. I don't know how, and I don't know why it took so long. He's not there anymore. His Phoenix genes finally kicked in or something. Quest will be reborn!"

My heart burst, and Falcon caught me before I slumped to the ground when my knees went weak. After everything we'd been through, my family remained whole. At least, I thought it did.

I spun in Falcon's arms to take in our army so I could find my children. They hadn't forced me to search them out. Cassius, Adler, and Garrett stood at the front of the large group. Each gave me a smile, and Adler waved.

Everyone else stared on, likely wondering what they were to do next, and if this was truly over. They didn't really need to witness my family time.

"We won! Go celebrate," I called into the crowd. "Just don't hurt anyone or use your abilities for darkness. I won't put up with that. Rest, mourn. Your leaders will be in touch shortly."

Cries of joy rose from the crowd. They hugged their neighbors, even if those neighbors had once been their enemies. Groups of Phoenixes and Darken rejoiced together. Some even slid away together. The only good thing to come from Chaos' time on Earth was the joining of our peoples. Some probably still held hate in their hearts, but the majority had begun to let go of past hurts for a better future.

My children all came forward and embraced each other. Garrett stood off to the side, unsure if he fit in with his siblings, but they pulled him into the group. Even Astrid was included, being mated to Quest, whom we all missed but would see again.

Falcon pulled me close to his side. "Well, they're all quite different, but they are all ours."

"And they're all wonderful." Love warmed my heart. The war with Chaos being over hadn't sunk in yet. We'd all live happy lives now. I prayed the peace between the Darken races and the Phoenixes would last, along with the peace amongst the Darken races.

Falcon tipped my chin up. His dark eyes began to smolder. "I think it's time I showed you how much I love you."

"I do not need to be here to hear this." Arlo grumbled and walked to our kids. My guess, he would try to woo Adler again now that the danger was passed. I wished him well. She might have helped him get back on his feet, but if he wanted her again, she'd make him work for it.

I placed my hand on Falcon's chest. His red eyes brightened when I leaned in and whispered, "I think I'm ready for you to show me just what I mean to you."

He grinned and his pointed canines made a shiver slide up my spine in anticipation. Falcon's face lowered to mine, his eyes never straying from my lips until his lips covered mine. His kiss was slow and tantalizing.

The sounds of rejoicing faded as Falcon slid. My back hit a cloud-like surface. Falcon pulled back enough I could make out his room at the house he'd first brought me to. From there on, the surroundings didn't have my attention as Falcon and I made new memories together that I would cherish for lifetimes.

CHAPTER 17

Falcon

"I feel like my boobs are getting bigger." I turned to find Brina in her panties while trying to clasp her bra.

Cassius had rebuilt the Shadow's tunnel home after the battle with Chaos. Circe hadn't lived through the attacks, but thankfully her spell had been strong enough to keep the children safe until Cassius could enforce his own spells upon the place.

"I like bigger."

She gave me a deadpan look after pausing her clasping efforts. "Could you just come help me?"

"Your breasts grew when you were pregnant," I threw out there nonchalantly as I relieved her of the clasps and finished the job she'd started. Mates should not be required to clasp bras.

"I can't be pregnant, though." Her cheeks brightened and she ducked her head. "I mean, it hasn't been very long since the first time, so..."

"We could practice making a baby again just to make sure it happens." She slapped my chest and walked into her closet. When she came back out, a modest black dress adorned her body. Blood revive me, I hated that dress.

"There's a meeting we're already late for, Falcon, and I am not, I repeat, I am *not*, having another awkward conversation between you and my father."

I chuckled as she went into the bathroom to do her hair. Irritating Brina was a delight, if only because she was a spitfire when she couldn't think of a reply fast enough, or I embarrassed her. I preferred the latter.

The fire in the fireplace flickered, drawing my attention to it. Again, the flames sputtered and nearly died. The chimney had been magicked to dispel the smoke the fire created. No air should come down the chimney to blow out the flames.

"Brina," I called to her as the flames died completely, leaving the hairs on the back of my neck standing up. Something wasn't right. Had Chaos returned somehow?

"Yeah… What happened to the fire?" Her slippered feet walked silently across the room to my side.

"I'm not sure. It just died out. Stay behind me." I pushed her behind me, ready to take on the danger which awaited us.

"Seriously? I'm the one who can be reborn."

"And you will not need to be reborn if I have anything to say about it. You've done that enough, and I refuse to allow you to go through such trauma again." As long as I lived, Brina would always breathe.

Flames sprung up from the fireplace, gold and blue, eating away at the wood as quickly as if it were paper.

"Oh my gosh," Brina breathed in awe. "I've never seen this before. Only heard the Griffins tell stories."

"What is it?"

"A rebirth, but the flames are supposed to be—"

The flames died as quickly as they'd come, leaving a naked little baby in the hearth. Brina squeaked out a sob while a large smile raised my lips. I knelt and picked up the white-haired infant. Brina rushed to her closet and returned with a throw blanket she used when she grew cool.

"He won't need that, darling. The cool air doesn't bother him."

Brina tutted as she took Quest from my arms and laid both him and the blanket on the bed to swaddle him. "Every baby loves to be held in a blanket."

As if to protest her thoughts, Quest let out a loud cry. Brina, who now held him, looked up at me with wide eyes. While she'd given birth to the boys, she'd never had the chance to care for them. I hadn't heard her speak about caring for a baby in any of her lives. My mate had no idea what to do with a crying infant, which brought a grin to my face.

"He's probably hungry."

"Well, um, when a Phoenix baby is reborn, the Griffin mom will start producing milk as if she were the baby's real mom. It's how the magic works." Brina put a hand on her chest. "That didn't feel nice."

"Your milk dropped."

"My what?"

"If Quest is reborn, his mom will start producing milk, no?"

"His Griffin mom."

"But Quest wasn't reborn to a Griffin. He's a Shadow and needs the darkness. So, he was reborn to us. Now, feed the boy."

Her mouth opened and closed as she bounced Quest. "But I have no idea how! And don't say it's natural, because I've heard the opposite from new moms. And stop laughing."

I couldn't help it. My mate was beautiful and fiery. Her panic was unwarranted. She would be the best mom she could be to our son. My heart sang for her, to finally have this chance to raise a baby of her own.

Her panic lessened. "We should tell Astrid."

"We'll tell her later."

"But she should be the one to take care of him. They are mates."

After nudging Brina to the bed, I helped her climb up with Quest and placed a pillow behind her. The baby wouldn't quit squawking until he had something in his belly, so I helped her from her dress and aided her in learning how to nurse him.

She'd never looked so sexy in her life, and she blushed when she caught me staring. "Turn around."

"No."

Ignoring me, Brina began talking to our baby. She told him all about how brave and smart Orion had been. She went on to tell him all about his siblings, how Adler and Arlo weren't back together yet, but Arlo wasn't planning on giving up; how Orion was on the search for Miriam, formerly known as Wraith; how Cassius was taking over the role of Conjurer First Four "like a pro"; and how Garrett was coming to terms with being the last of his kind. She even informed him that he'd better brace himself, because Astrid would probably kill him when he matured for scaring her to death.

Quest gave her some nice burps when she'd finished feeding him. He wet the blanket, and Brina called for me to go buy diapers. I still wasn't perfect, but I did leave some cash from where I took the diapers from the shelf in the department store.

With Brina dressed in jammies and Quest in a clean diaper and new outfit I'd snagged as well, I sent off a message to Keeve that we would be missing the meeting. We'd explain later, but all was well. And no, it wasn't to make love, though I did plan for that to happen soon.

"Quick, Falc, use your phone to take a picture." I looked up to find Quest holding Brina's finger in a tight grip. The smile on her face was dazzling.

"We don't need a picture."

"But humans take loads of pictures when their babies are born." Brina bent down and kissed Quest's little hand. "And I don't want to forget this moment."

As she stared down into the eyes of our Shadow son, I fell harder for her than I ever had before. And when she put it that way, I had no choice but to pull out my phone and take a picture with her and our precious son. Brina would always remember the moments she wanted to. I'd make sure of it.

As I scrolled back through the photos I'd taken while Brina spoke childishly to the baby, my heart squeezed. The candid photos of them were everything.

She looked up at me. "We really should tell Astrid so she can relax."

"Agreed, but you were given him to raise. And you will raise him. Astrid can help, but you are his mother. She can wait to have him for forever after giving you a few years."

Brina smiled down at the baby now asleep in her arms. "Mommy and Daddy won't let anything happen to you. You're safe with us."

Inwardly, I promised Brina the same. She would not go through pain as long as I lived and breathed. A deep part of my mind brought an ugly thought forward. With Chaos out of the picture, what kind of Darken would the evil in the world bring us next? Whatever it was, I would protect my family from such darkness and evil. My mate would never suffer again, and our children, current and future, would enjoy being loved by their beautiful mother.

~

Thanks for reading "Return to Haunt"! I'd appreciate your time if you could take a few moments and leave a review. Also, let me know if you want more stories in the "Things That Go Bump" world!

ALSO BY MELANIE GILBERT

A Fae Brothers' Ever Afters Series

Midnight: A Cinderella Retelling

Enchanted: A Beauty and the Beast Retelling

Captive: A Rapunzel Retelling

Poison: A Snow White Retelling

Deal: A Rumpelstiltskin Retelling

Deception: A Hansel and Gretel Retelling

Greed: A Christmas Carol Retelling

Oath: A Goose Girl Retelling

Things That Go Bump

Bump in the Night

The Witching Hour

Return to Haunt

Sons of Water

Elemental Assassin

Elemental Warrior

Elemental Destroyer

Elemental Prisoner

Elemental Healer

Elemental Traitor

Dark Night Series

Dark of the Night

Blood of the Night

Blood and Magic Series

Blood and Dust

Bites and Bonds

Hunt and Seek

Standalones

Alpha King

The Curse of Thorn

Sowing Catastrophe

Of Fishes and Wishes

Something Wicked

If you'd like to stay up to date on releases subscribe to our newsletter at www.scribblingpenpublishing.com!

ABOUT THE AUTHOR

Melanie Gilbert is an award-winning author who is addicted to hot chocolate and writing. Seriously, she can't stop writing the words or guzzling gallons of hot chocolate a year like a Christmas elf. When she's not writing, Melanie enjoys long walks where she spends the entire time plotting and talking her husband's ear off about plots. Currently, the beautiful state of Wisconsin is her home where she lives with her hubby, two kiddos, and puppy, Link.

CONNECT WITH SCRIBBLING PEN PUBLISHING

www.scribblingpenpublishing.com
Facebook: Scribbling Pen Publishing
Facebook Street Team: Scribbling Pen Publishing Street Team
Instagram @scribblingpenpublishing

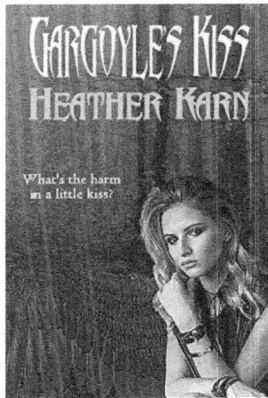

Gargoyle's Kiss by Heather Karn

What's the harm in a little kiss?

Gargoyles: the ugly, mutant creatures atop prestigious old buildings. Statues and tales, not flesh and blood men. When Larissa accidentally kisses one of the statues, everything she knows of gargoyles is tossed on its head.

It isn't long before Aeron, the attractive gargoyle Lari kissed, shows up at her apartment to tell her that she's his new mate. If that wasn't enough, his news that the gargoyle's curse now falls on her leaves dread curling in Lari's stomach.

Can Larissa survive her new life of demons and curses while trying not to fall in love with a gargoyle?

http://mybook.to/GargoylesKiss

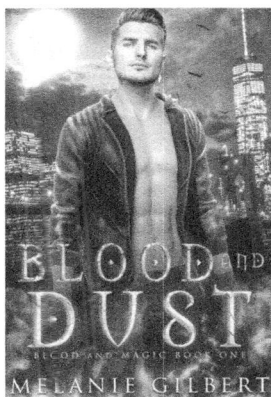

Blood and Dust by Melanie Gilbert

Even the villain will do the right thing...for the wrong reason.

Vampires are driven by blood, and Gabriel Zach is no exception. In over one hundred years, he's never smelled anything as divine and exquisite as the blood of vampire hunter, Lennon Stewart. And he's never met anyone who drives his lust through the roof quite like her.

But Gabe isn't the only monster who's attracted to Lennon's scent. An attack by a mysterious monster leaves the hunter in the arms of her worst enemy: Gabriel, the vampire stalking her. If he's not strong enough, he'll devour her before he's ready.

Lennon's job is to kill monsters, but Gabe's job is to keep her alive, if only for selfish purposes. At the end of the day, will both make it to sunrise alive?

https://books2read.com/u/bORpDA

Made in the USA
Monee, IL
25 October 2023